I0687139

Mirror Shattered

KG Stutts

Published by Distinguished Press
Cover by The Writing Network
Copyright 2014; 2015
ISBN 978-1-63310-016-9
ISBN 978-1-63310-003-9

Mirror Shattered

CHAPTER ONE

Maddie and John Brooks sat out on a blanket in the park near their house. It was a beautiful Sunday afternoon in Charleston, without a cloud in the sky. In the distance, they could hear their two-year-old son, Lucas, playing with Maddie's best friend, Mallory.

"What are you thinking?" John asked Maddie as he popped a grape into his mouth.

"How perfect this is," Maddie answered.

She closed her eyes, feeling the gentle breeze of the warm, spring day. Her long blonde hair mingled in the grass, framing her beautiful heart shaped face as the sun warmed her skin. John curled up beside her, nuzzling her neck. His kisses traced her jaw, nipping tenderly on her with his teeth. He gently flipped Maddie onto her back as he kissed her, strands of his copper hair falling in his eyes. Lucas chose that moment to burst through the grass toward his parents. His little arms were stretched out wide, giggling, as he crashed into his father. Lucas' dirty blonde hair fell into his blue eyes as he snuggled against John's chest.

"You sure know how to ruin a moment, son." John scooped up the toddler in his arms.

"Daddy, come play!" Lucas encouraged.

Mallory came running up gasping for air. She paused, with her hands on her knees, to catch her breath.

"Sorry, guys. This little guy got away from me," Mallory stated.

"Daddy, *come* play!"

The toddler wiggled out of his father's arms and was now pulling on his hand toward the swings. Maddie blew her husband a kiss before the two walked off.

"Those two are a handful," Mallory said, taking a seat beside Maddie.

"Yeah, but in the best kind of way." Maddie smiled.

"Hard to believe just less than three years ago, you were this lonely girl working in a dead end job."

"In your eyes." Maddie rolled her eyes, popping a grape in her mouth.

"Well, now look at you. You have a great job now, back in the field you love and belong in. You have a wonderful husband and a great son. Thinking about having any more children?"

"The thought has crossed our minds, but Lucas was such a difficult delivery. The doctor told me he doubts I could conceive again. We have talked about adopting though." Maddie smiled as she watched John and Lucas play.

"I envy you."

"You and Kyle will get there," Maddie said, giving her friend's hand a squeeze. Mallory had been trying to get pregnant for nearly a year and was beginning to lose hope.

"I hope so. You make it seem so easy. It's like this is what you were made for."

"Yeah, not bad for a small town girl from Ladson." Maddie grinned, closing her eyes as another gust of wind hit her face. She breathed in the spring air, feeling all was well with this life they had created.

#

"Catching up on the news from home?" a voice asked Maddie from behind.

"It's my favorite TV show," Maddie said, not looking up from her computer monitor.

"Clone TV." The voice joked.

"Something like that."

"Well, hate to disturb you, but I got that report you requested."

Maddie ended the video feed before turning off her monitor and turned around. Her assistant, Hunter Lewis, stood behind her, holding out a manila folder.

"Thanks. It took longer than expected," Maddie said sternly, accepting the folder.

"I'm sorry. It was trickier than I originally thought," Hunter stammered.

"It's fine."

Hunter pressed his lips into a thin line. Something was bothering her. It was unlike Maddie to be so dismissive toward him.

"You must be pleased. Latest tests show the satellites are functioning above expectations," Hunter commented, trying to lure Maddie into a conversation.

"You mean for their age?" Maddie questioned as she raised an eyebrow.

"Two years without needing maintenance is impressive."

"Hmm." Maddie went back to reading the report.

After a few minutes, Hunter cleared his throat.

"Can I help you with something?" she asked without looking up.

"Are you okay, Boss?" Hunter asked.

"I'm fine."

"Did I do something wrong?"

"You mean, other than bringing me this report three hours late?"

"Is that what's bothering you?"

"Go away, Hunter."

Hunter fell silent, but Maddie could still feel his eyes on her. She sighed heavily and looked up at her young assistant. He was tall and skinny, with a shock of bright red hair and green eyes. His cheeks and nose was dotted with freckles and he had started to grow out a goatee.

"What is it?" Maddie asked.

"If you are fine, and I haven't done anything wrong, what is eating you?"

"Hunter, I'm really not in the mood," Maddie snapped.

"I see this. Why?"

Maddie glared, knowing he would continue to annoy her until he got a satisfying answer. She placed her report on her table and rubbed her temples.

"John isn't back yet," she told him.

"Ah, so you are worried."

"He was supposed to be back two days ago. I've been praying for some news but so far…"

Angst was etched across Maddie's face as her stomach turned into knots. Her husband, John, went off-world with her counterpart, Mack, two weeks ago. Last communication they had was four days ago.

"I'm sure he's fine. Have you heard from Mack?" Hunter asked.

"If I had, do you think I would be worried?"

"Oh, good point, with Mack being the pilot and all..." Hunter's voice trailed off.

"For a genius, you can be quite dumb," Maddie said crossly.

"Okay, you are upset, so I'm not going to take offense to that."

Maddie scoffed and rolled her eyes.

"I'm sure they are fine," Hunter gently said.

"If they were, they would have been home by now." Maddie frowned.

"Boss, would you like a hug?"

"What? Oh, good God, no." Maddie backed up, giving him a dirty look.

"Come on, bring it in," Hunter encouraged, outstretching his pale, skinny arms.

"I will hit you," Maddie warned.

"And it will hurt. Come on, Boss." Hunter took a step toward her.

"Don't," Maddie warned him again.

She tried to keep a stern look on her face. Hunter took another step toward her, and she lost it. Maddie couldn't help but laugh. As soon as she laughed, Hunter wrapped his arms around her. She, in turn, gave him a big hug.

"All right, all right. That's enough." Maddie pushed against his chest.

"Not so bad, was it?"

"Thanks," she said before punching him in the shoulder.

"Ow! What was that for?" Hunter asked, rubbing his shoulder.

"I told you I would hit you."

"I could report you to Commander Westlake," he grumbled.

"Go ahead." Maddie shrugged. "You'll just end up reassigned. And I can guarantee that no one is as much fun as I am."

Hunter pretended to think about it, his eyes swinging up to look at the ceiling as he rocked back on his heels.

"You win this time," Hunter wagged his finger at her before crossing his arms over his chest. She raised an eyebrow at him, leaning her head to the side. His stern expression dropped off as he beamed at her. "Can't fool you for a second."

"Nope."

Maddie smiled at her young assistant. Like her, Hunter graduated high school at a young age. He had gotten his Masters from M.I.T. at the age of nineteen. Now, at twenty-three, he had been a big help to her as she started working on new software for the ISC's ships. There was no doubt about how smart Hunter was, but he always acted like a teenager. He loved joking around and having fun in the lab. His twin sister was more serious and grounded. No wonder Mack chose Morgan as her assistant.

The intercom in her office buzzed, alerting her that her presence was requested in the hangar.

"Ask and you shall receive." Hunter smiled.

Maddie jumped from her chair, giddy that John was getting ready to land.

"Thanks, kid," she said, patting him gently on the shoulder she punched earlier.

"Anytime, Boss."

#

Maddie ran out of her office, nearly colliding with Jackson in the hallway. They raced each other to the hangar, which Maddie won by a narrow margin. Mack and John had landed and were talking to Commander Charlie Westlake when they entered.

"Excuse me," John told the Commander.

He rushed toward Maddie, swinging her up in his arms in an embrace.

"I've missed you," she said into his neck.

"I've missed you."

"Two days, John?"

"We ran into a little fire on the way home. The ship suffered some damage, took out communications. Nothing that Mack couldn't handle," he explained.

Maddie looked over at the other couple, smiling as Mack shook her short, pixie-like hair from her helmet before hugging her husband, Jackson. She gave her counterpart a little wave before turning back to John.

John's blue eyes danced as he brushed back a clump of his copper hair. His thumb lightly grazed her cheek before meeting her lips again.

Without saying another word, John scooped up Maddie and tossed her over his shoulder.

"We'll see everyone later," John announced with a wave.

"Put me down!" Maddie yelled.

John chuckled and gave her a playful smack on her rear in response.

"We have a debriefing meeting in thirty minutes, Agent Brooks!" Commander Westlake called to him.

"Give me an hour." John waved as he left the hangar.

"One hour, I mean it!"

John walked effortlessly down the corridor of the ISC with Maddie over his shoulder, not caring about the looks he was getting from other agents.

"John, this is embarrassing. Let me go!" Maddie insisted.

"Not on your life."

John carried Maddie into their apartment. She laughed as he tossed her onto the bed. He quickly disrobed and climbed into bed with her.

"You are way overdressed for what I have in mind," he teased.

Maddie gave her husband a playful look as she got undressed. When he reached for her again, time seemed to lose all meaning. The only thing holding her focus was his body, his scent overriding her senses as they got lost in each other.

It wasn't until his communicator cuff on his wrist started beeping that they were snapped out of their private bubble.

"What happened to giving me an hour?" John spoke gruffly into the cuff.

"It's been over an hour, Agent Brooks," Commander Westlake responded.

"Oh, shit." John jumped up from the bed.

Maddie licked her lips as she watched him get dressed. John caught the hungry look in her eyes as he reached for his shirt.

"I'm not done with you yet," he promised.

"Hurry back," she encouraged.

John bent down and kissed her. Maddie playfully nibbled on his bottom lip.

"Woman, you are going to get me into trouble."

"How about I just make you come unglued instead?" Maddie teasingly said.

"Now, Agent Brooks," Commander Westlake bellowed from the communicator.

"Later," John promised.

CHAPTER TWO

Maddie was bent over her workbench with her magnifying glasses on. Several computer components were scattered in front of her as she worked to attach a tiny piece to a motherboard.

"Hey," John said, sitting down at the bench.

"Almost done." Maddie didn't look up as she spoke.

"Hurry up, Maddie. I'm hungry."

Maddie stayed focused on her task and didn't respond.

"What are you working on anyway?" he asked.

"This will be a long distance camera that is capable of self-maintenance," Maddie explained.

"Wow, you can do that?"

"There isn't much I can't do with a few computer parts."

"I have the weather analysis for you, Boss," Hunter said, walking up to the table.

"On my desk," Maddie instructed.

"Weather analysis? In space?" John questioned. "Isn't that usually the same?"

"I just need it for the math variables on the self-sustaining system," Maddie explained.

"Oh, I've got the blood results for you, too," Hunter said.

"Very good," Maddie said, putting down her instrument and taking off her magnifying glasses.

"Blood results? What are you working on?" John questioned.

"This has to do with the cloning program," Maddie responded.

"Cloning program? Just how many projects do you have going on?" John asked.

"Uh .. .what would you say, Hunter? Five?"

"Six," Hunter corrected.

"Oh, right. Yeah, six."

After Maddie joined the ISC two years ago, Commander Westlake asked her for assistance with the cloning program. Maddie had proved a lot of things they believed about clones to be wrong, and they both wanted answers. The best way to get that was to get her involved.

She was skeptical at first. After all, her level of expertise was in theoretical physics and engineering, but curiosity got the better of her. She didn't know what she was doing, initially. Thanks to assistance from Hunter and the head of the cloning department, Dr. Wayne Brody, she soon got a firm grasp on the process. It helped if she looked at the DNA code like computer software.

Maddie took the flash drive from Hunter and plugged it into her computer. She pulled up the report that showed the breakdown of her blood cells compared to her counterpart, Mack.

She had to read the report several times to make sure she understood it correctly.

"This can't be right," Maddie said in disbelief after a few minutes.

"I got it from the lab myself," Hunter stiffly said.

"No, Hunter. I'm not saying you did something wrong." Maddie shook her head. "But this can't be right."

"What's up?" John asked, peaking over her shoulder.

"The left side of the screen is mine." Maddie pointed to the monitor.

"Maddie, I'm a soldier, not a scientist. You and Hunter may be able to read this, but I'm not sure what I'm looking at."

Maddie ran her tongue over the bottom of her lip before letting out a haggard breath. She wasn't positive she was right, but would do her best to explain it to him as she saw it.

"Cells divide and break down over age and time. It's a natural process of aging," Maddie began.

"Although it's hard to say for sure. The link between chronological and cellular age is different," Hunter pointed out.

"Cellular age can differ when you factor in health behaviors," Maddie countered. "But you can't deny that the two fall in line."

"Okay, Maddie ... I'm a little lost here," John interrupted, looking at them confused.

"Sorry. As I was saying before I was rudely interrupted," Maddie shot a glare over to her assistant, "cells divide and die as they get older and are replaced by other cells. The dead cells can leave behind a little marker. It can show the age of the blood, the cells, and the tissues affected."

"Right, I'm sort of following." John nodded.

"Well, according to this, mine shows the natural cell growth and death associated with a woman in her thirties. Mack's show what would be more common with someone much younger in age," Maddie explained.

John and Hunter both paused, trying to process what Maddie just said.

"Layman's terms, Maddie," John said.

"If this is correct, I'm older than Mack," Maddie slowly said.

Her words hung in the air as the seemingly impossible fact washed over them.

"How is that possible? Forgive me, Boss, but aren't you the clone?" Hunter blurted out the question.

"According to these test results, no, I'm not."

Maddie studied the blood cells again, stroking her chin in thought. She rubbed her temples and eyes, trying to make sense of all of it in her head.

This couldn't be possible. It had to be a mistake. Maybe a lab technician swapped the blood samples or mislabeled them?

Two years ago, she received the news which would alter her life. She was a clone. Now, lab evidence was telling her it wasn't true. What the hell was going on?

Her mind raced back to when she was first told she was a clone. Jackson had plucked her from work, after an alien race, the Gorium, fired at her. She later helped save Jackson from a rogue agent hell-bent on revenge against Mack and found out that a shape-shifter had taken the place of their commanding officer, Charlie. The same shape-shifter took her right arm, trying to figure out a way to duplicate her to create an army of clones.

She rubbed the spot on her shoulder where her robotic replacement arm met living tissue. She was almost killed because it was thought that she was unique from other clones. Every day, she was reminded of the torture that she endured. Every day, she became increasingly grateful for the silicon covering that acted as skin to her right arm. No one could tell by looking at her that there was a difference in her limbs.

She would have been disassembled piece by piece if it hadn't been for John. She looked into his blue eyes, watching the raging storm in them. John, the love of her life, whom she was originally told was impossible for her to love. Clones weren't capable of forming attachments, other than ones present at the time of creation. Yet Maddie loved him with all her heart. She didn't meet John or his clone until after she was supposedly created. Her counterpart, Mack, was already in love and married to Jackson when they met.

Several years of her life, she had lived a lie. Seven now, if she counted the five years prior that Mack had been with the ISC.

"Is it possible that you aren't looking at it correctly?" Hunter questioned. "I mean, this isn't exactly your forte."

"Of course it's always possible. I'm far from infallible," Maddie said, ignoring the dig from her assistant.

She had to prove that a mistake had been made. It was the only logical explanation, right? She would do the only thing she could think of. She needed to examine her blood herself.

Maddie grabbed a syringe from a medical bag she had under a cabinet and drew blood from her human left arm.

"Ugh, this is too gross this close to lunch," Hunter complained.

"Man up," Maddie sharply said.

She placed a tiny amount of blood into a test tube and put it in a centrifuge, a machine that spun around to separate the cells. After that, Maddie ran the new sample through amass spectrometer.

The three of them remained silent as they waited for the analysis to be complete. All she could think of was either a mistake had been made when Hunter gave them the original specimens, or a different kind of mistake had occurred seven years ago.

So which was it?

The machine printed out the results, giving her the cellular details. She gave John a small smile before scanning over the paper. Her breath caught in her throat as she compared the print out to the computer file. The results matched the report Hunter had given her.

She still couldn't believe it. She had to be reading it incorrectly. Maddie knew the only way she was going to get real answers was to go to the source. She needed to speak with Dr. Wayne Brody.

"If you are hungry, you may need to go to the mess hall without me," Maddie told John.

"I suddenly lost my appetite," John said, shaking his head.

#

"Good afternoon, Maddie," Dr. Brody greeted warmly as Maddie, John, and Hunter marched into his office. He didn't seem bothered at all by her intrusion or take notice to the two men flanking her.

Maddie really liked Dr. Brody. He was an older man, approximately in his late sixties. His short hair had turned white many years ago. He wore wire thin glasses that made his light blue eyes shine brightly and his white beard was always well groomed. Dr. Brody always seemed to be in a good mood that was infectious.

"Dr. Brody, I have a few questions," Maddie started.

"Of course, my dear. You know I'm happy to help. Such an eager mind." Dr. Brody smiled at her.

"I had Hunter run a blood analysis level on myself and Mack, and I don't think I understand the results."

"That's your problem, Maddie." Dr. Brody's smile widened. "You have a brilliant mind, but you always seem to doubt yourself. I'm sure you understood it fine."

"No, sir, I really don't think so."

Maddie was suddenly nervous. Her entire body started to shake as she noticed the smile was still there on his lips, but his eyes seemed to change.

"All right, Maddie. Show me what you mean, and I'll be happy to explain it."

Maddie handed him the print out from the earlier lab results. Automatically, his eyes squinted, his lips pressed together as he pushed the glasses up the bridge of his nose.

"There had to be some mistake, Maddie. I'm sure some assistant labeled it wrong," Dr. Brody dismissively said.

"See, I thought the same thing at first, but then I ran a test myself from my left arm." She handed him the other print out.

Dr. Brody's smile dropped off fast. His hands seemed to shake as he took the other report from her, comparing the results with the first spreadsheet.

"Oh, hell. I always said it was a bad idea for you to get involved with the cloning program. I told

Charlie you shouldn't be researching anything to do with it."

"You mean these results are accurate?" Hunter asked.

"Yes, Mr. Lewis. The lab tech had orders to switch the names on the vials. Guess that didn't happen."

Dr. Brody could have been talking about the weather, as offhandedly as he admitted to ordering the results to be switched.

Maddie gasped at the confirmation. Her body shook violently as the room began to spin. Her knees began to buckle but John caught her and helped her to a chair. Hunter dart out of the room and brought her a glass of water.

"Madison..."

"No!" John snapped, turning his attention away from his wife to advance on the doctor. "You don't get to talk right now."

"John..." Maddie's voice was barely above a whisper.

Whatever anger and resentment he felt toward the elderly man he swallowed so he could tend to his wife. John took off his jacket and wrapped it around Maddie, who was still shaking. He pressed his hands to the side of her face, forcing her to meet his eyes.

"You're okay," he told her.

She shook her head slightly, swallowing hard.

"Listen to me." John's rough voice called through the haze in her mind. "You are still the same woman I love and have been with the last two years. This doesn't change anything."

Two years. It could have been seven.

Maddie's brain refused to formulate words. Her body was still in too much shock to comprehend anything. John hugged her to his chest, stroking her long blonde hair and whispering encouraging words to her. After a few minutes, her nails slightly grazed his shoulders as she slowly started to return.

"You're okay," John repeated.

"I'm okay," she confirmed, her voice shaking slightly.

She gradually turned her attention back to the doctor, whose eyes filled with tears as he looked at her. "I'm not the clone." She was surprised at how strong her voice sounded.

"No, my dear. You're not. Mack is."

"Why didn't you say something?" Maddie asked.

"I was too afraid." Dr. Brody's voice was so soft, it was barely above a whisper.

"Afraid? I'll give you something to be afraid of, old man." John's face started to turn red.

John balled up his fists, the muscles in his arms straining against his shirt. Before Hunter or Maddie could stop him, John tossed the scientist over his own desk, papers, and personal objects scattering on the floor.

"John!" Maddie cried out, using the strength in her robotic arm to pull John from the doctor.

He let out a low growl as Hunter helped her back John off. She placed a gentle hand on his shoulder, trying to calm him down. She understood his anger. She was beginning to feel it, too, but what she wanted more than anything right now was answers.

"I need to know, and if you knock him out, he won't be able to tell us," she calmly stated.

John breathed out deeply, doing everything he could to control his temper. Maddie slid her left hand in his, giving him a small squeeze.

Dr. Brody cleared his throat as he managed to stand up straight, taking off his glasses to wipe them on his handkerchief. Maddie noticed the bead of sweat forming on his brow.

"Are you okay, Dr. Brody?" Hunter asked.

John's steel gaze followed the doctor around the room, who pushed away from his desk and turned his back to the group.

"Wayne, what happened?" Maddie gently asked.

The pit of her stomach twisted when he didn't answer her. She walked over to him, slowly turning his shoulder to make him face her. When he looked at her, tears were freely spilling from his gentle blue eyes.

"I'm so sorry," Dr. Brody sobbingly said.

"You can tell us," Hunter gently coaxed.

Maddie looked over at her assistant who looked torn between anger and sympathy. She gave him a weak smile before looking back at the doctor.

"No, I can't." He shook his head.

"Wayne, please tell me," Maddie begged. "I've got to know what happened."

"Madison, I am so sorry. I can't. If I tell you, it could cost me everything."

"What happened? Please, please tell me. I've got to know the truth."

The doctor wiped the tears from his face and tried to compose himself.

"The truth? For what I am about to tell you, please don't hate me. And don't tell Mack," Dr. Brody started.

"Okay." Maddie agreed.

"Promise me, Madison." Dr. Brody gripped her hands tightly, only releasing her when she nodded.

"I promise."

Dr. Brody took a deep breath and let it out slowly.

"I remember the day clearly. I still go over it in my head every night before I fall to sleep. You were brought into my office by Charlie so we could begin the necessary tests ... You looked so frightened. You had on this light purple shirt and matching purple ribbon at the end of a long braid." Wayne smiled briefly at the memory.

"I did?" Maddie asked, clearly not remembering.

"You did. You had just undergone orientation and had decided you were ready to have your clone created. You talked to me for a long time about your family. It made me feel like I knew them."

Her family back in Charleston. Mom, Dad, her brother Noah, Noah's twin children, her best friend Mallory...

Perhaps she should be grateful she had five more years with them than Mack did. But those were the five years Mack, in theory, should've had with them. Seemed like a selfish thought, all things considered.

"Anyway, when it came time to copy your memories, there was a ... snafu."

"A snafu?" John questioned.

"Maddie's memories were confused with that of the clones. Instead of the built memories I created going into the clone, they went to Madison. The real Madison. You."

"Me." Maddie swallowed the hard lump forming in her throat.

"Yes, my dear. But I realized my mistake too late. You were already back home without your memory of the agency, of me, of any of it."

"I'm sorry, how does a mistake like this happen?" John demanded.

Dr. Brody sighed. "The memory part of the cloning development is a complicated process. It's as difficult as the actual formation of the clone itself. The creation of the false memories is a very delicate and intricate operation. It takes time and must be handled with care," he explained.

"And, what, you failed to handle with care?" Venom dripped from John's voice.

"That's right, I did not," he replied.

"I don't understand, sir," Hunter piped up from behind.

"No, Mr. Lewis, I suppose you wouldn't," Dr. Brody said.

"So what happened?" Maddie asked.

"It seems so simple looking back. Had I just double checked my work, this wouldn't have happened."

Maddie bit her lip, feeling her body start to shake again. A simple mathematical mistake. It could have happened to anyone. It just so happened this simple gaffe not only affected her and Mack, but John and Jackson as well.

The three of them fell silent, waiting on Dr. Brody to continue.

"The memories are the final stage of the cloning process. Once it is ready, the clone and the counterpart are hooked up to a machine to complete the transfer. Memories from the agent are pulled and processed through a computer and transferred into the newly-created clone, and then the false memories are placed. Only this time, once the memories were pulled from Madison, something peculiar happened. The memories failed to correctly integrate into the false ones I had created. Somehow, all Madison's memories were transferred into the clone, leaving behind the memories intended for the clone. The memories intended for the clone went to Madison instead."

"How did that happen?" Hunter asked. "I still don't understand.

"It was my fault, Mr. Lewis. I programmed the system in error. I didn't catch the mistake until it was too late. Mack was fully integrated into the agency, and Maddie was back home." Dr. Brody hung his head in shame.

Maddie sat in silence, her mind processing the new information. So that answered one lingering question of how she was able to perform above what the agency expected of her. But in the same regard, Mack would have blown any expectation they had for clones out of the water.

"Wayne, this doesn't make sense to me," Maddie spoke up after a few moments.

"Ah, connecting the dots, are you?"

"Connecting what dots?" Hunter asked.

"If Mack is a clone, how is she able to do, well, everything that Mack does?" Maddie asked.

"This is where my mistake just gets worse. I decided to try to turn my blunder into something positive. Mack became something for me."

"What exactly did you do?" Maddie raised an eyebrow as she placed her hands on her hips.

"I always thought clones could be more than what we allowed them to be, and it was my chance to prove it. So I talked her back into my lab to make some ... modifications."

"Modifications? Is that what you call it?" John asked, raising his voice.

Maddie felt John's body go rigid next to her, knowing he was close to exploding again. She gently ran her hand up his arm, willing him to calm down. She had to let Dr. Brody get out his explanations.

"I wanted to help perfect the cloning process, and this was my chance. So, yes, modifications. I was able to put her to sleep for a while and modify her to the person we know and love today," Dr. Brody explained.

"You manipulated her!" Maddie exclaimed.

This time it was John who held Maddie back. Wayne scrambled to get out of her reach as she clawed and kicked in his direction.

"Hey, I know," John soothingly said, cupping her chin. "You're hurt and angry and believe me, there's nothing I would rather see than you kicking his ass."

"Then let me go." Maddie growled.

"Madison, I'm sorry," Dr. Brody softly said. "You promised you wouldn't hate me."

"Hey," John's voice commanded her attention back to him. "I get how you feel, but you're right. Beat him up after we get the whole story," John said with a sly grin.

"Better listen to what he has to say, Boss," Hunter encouraged.

Maddie snorted through her nose, her lips twitching slightly. After a second, she returned John's grin. They both knew she wouldn't have it in her to get into a physical confrontation after she calmed down. John knew her well enough that even though she was justifiably angry, she would feel guilty for her actions later.

Maddie leaned in and kissed the tip of John's nose, muttering a word of thanks before nodding over to the doctor for him to continue.

"I only brought out the traits in her that I see you, Madison. You are a great engineer and probably one of the smartest people I have ever met. You ought to have 'doctor' attached to your name. However, you were always more suited for the lab than the field. But I saw something in you which I believed I could bring out in your clone. I took fear out of her. I gave her the opportunity to be a leader. I kept your ability to love with all the passions your heart has. I gave her a life most could only dream of. I unlocked things in her no clone was ever allowed to have." Passion resonated in Dr. Brody's voice.

"And you never told her," John dryly said.

"Of course not. She believed that she was Madison Mackenzie Rhodes and, thanks to me, she was. She is," Dr. Brody defended.

"Who else knows about this?" Hunter asked.

"Not another soul. I changed my computer files to hide any evidence."

"So you knew what you did was wrong," Maddie coolly said.

"I merely fixed an error. I didn't do anything wrong," he defended.

"No, sir. If you truly believed you didn't do anything wrong, you wouldn't have hidden it. You wouldn't have lied," Maddie countered.

"You told us that if it got out, you would lose everything," John pointed out.

"Justify it all you want, Dr. Brody, but you knew you should've come clean with what happened," Maddie spat.

Maddie backed away from the doctor in disgust.

"You really should own up for your mistakes and face the consequences. I'm going to Charlie and put your fate in his hands. Just be grateful that's all I'm doing."

"Madison, please don't do this. I was afraid that if Charlie knew what happened, he would think of both of you as a security risk. I didn't want to lose you."

Maddie couldn't take it anymore. She gave him a look of pure revulsion and left his office.

She heard Dr. Brody call to her, but she ignored him. John and Hunter trailed behind her, but she did not make any attempt to stop her stride. She stormed into Commander Charlie Westlake's office without knocking.

#

"Charlie, I just came from Dr. --" Maddie stopped in mid-sentence as her jaw dropped open.

Charlie's normally organized office was in chaos. Pictures and diplomas which normally hung on the walls were crammed in boxes. An agent was clearing out the desk, carelessly packing its contents in a large box. The filing cabinet was open with papers spilling out of it onto the floor. Charlie sat in the corner in his large office chair, looking despondent. He looked older, somehow. As if the day's events made him age suddenly.

"What's going on?" Maddie's heated tone instantly dissipated.

"I'm being replaced." Charlie stared at the wall, not glancing in her direction as he spoke.

"Replaced?"

Charlie didn't say anything as she walked over to him and placed a hand on his shoulder. She got down on one knee and slowly turned his chair to face her. His normally warm eyes stared right through her for a moment. A loud crash from the agent dropping a picture frame got his attention.

"You be careful with my things!"

"What's going on here?" John asked as he rushed into the office with Hunter close behind on his heels.

"Charlie is being replaced," Maddie informed as she stood up to stand next to her husband as they watching the scene in shock.

"Replaced? By whom?" John asked.

"By me," a woman's voice answered from behind.

Startled, Maddie and John turned to face the woman. She was slightly taller than Maddie, with long jet black hair framing her oval face and striking green eyes. She appeared to be a few years younger than Maddie. Her thin lips were pressed together in a scowl upon seeing John, who let out a gasp, color fading from his face.

The other woman's eyes looked somehow extremely familiar. *How did these two know each other?*

"Well, well, well. Somehow, I just knew I would run into you," she mused sardonically, her gaze fixed on John.

John hadn't recovered from his shock. He stood agape, staring at the young woman. Maddie looked over at John and then at Hunter, who appeared to be completely flabbergasted as his eyes darted back and forth. She tossed her hair over her shoulder, trying to quickly regain her composure.

"I'm sorry," Maddie stated, looking over at John to the other woman. "My name is Madison. Well, Maddie for short," she introduced, holding out her hand.

"I'm aware of who you are," the woman replied sternly, ignoring Maddie's offering of a handshake.

"Oh." Maddie bit her lip as she dropped her hand.

The woman looked at her with such disregard. *How could this woman hate me so much already?*

"What's the matter, John? Cat got your tongue?" the woman questioned bitterly.

"Elizabeth? Can that really be you?" John finally asked.

"Oh, so you do remember?" Elizabeth raised an eyebrow.

"Elizabeth? As in, your little sister?" Maddie questioned, her eyes widening.

"I'm surprised you have heard of me," Elizabeth said, her voice emotionless.

"Of course I've heard of John's sister." Maddie attempted to keep her voice from faltering.

"I didn't know John had a sister," Hunter commented.

"I guess you could call me that. We do technically do share a bloodline. I'm Elizabeth Levette."

Maddie was taken aback by the younger woman's resentment. John didn't seem to notice it. Before she could inquire about it, John threw his arms around his sister.

"I never thought I would see you again." His words were broken by emotion. Maddie didn't have to see his face to know that he was crying.

"Save it," Elizabeth bitterly said, shoving her brother away from her.

"What?" John blinked twice, stunned by her reaction.

"I don't want to hear it. Just …" Elizabeth paused for a moment. "Save your lies. I don't want to hear it."

"It's not a lie. I searched and searched for you for years. Seth and Logan did, too. None of us could find a single trace of you, Elizabeth. If I had known where you were, I would have come for you," John defended.

Elizabeth snorted, obviously unmoved.

"Whatever you say, *brother*." Elizabeth practically spat out the last word.

"So your sister is our new Commander?" Hunter asked.

"I am," Elizabeth stiffly responded.

"Charlie, what's going on?" Maddie questioned, turning away from the siblings.

"I would have you address your questions to me, thank you," Elizabeth intervened.

"I'm sorry, Maddie." Charlie shook his head.

"Charles Westlake has been found unfit to keep command, Ms. Rhodes," Elizabeth stated.

"Found unfit? By whom? And call me Maddie."

"Ms. Rhodes," Elizabeth corrected. "Charles Westlake has been removed from his position effective immediately."

"Immediately?"

"Yes, immediately, Ms. Rhodes." Elizabeth narrowed her eyes, obviously not happy about having to repeat herself.

"If you insist on calling me anything other than Maddie, then my name would be Mrs. Brooks," Maddie sharply replied. Two could play the disgruntled game.

"Ms. Rhodes, I do not recognize your marriage to Agent Brooks."

"Excuse me?" John and Maddie asked in unison.

"You," Elizabeth pointed at Maddie. "are a clone. You should not be a part of this agency."

Maddie was shocked beyond belief. This woman was not only angry at John for some unknown reason but at her as well.

"But Maddie is not a clone." John narrowed his eyes and balled up his fists in frustration.

"What?"

"We just came from Dr. Brody's office. There was a mistake in the lab the day that the clone was created. I'm not the clone," Maddie informed her.

Elizabeth paused, looking at her in disbelief. She raised an eyebrow before giving her a simple shrug.

"I'm going to need to see evidence of this. Until then, Ms. Rhodes has been removed from duty. She is to be escorted to her quarters and await further instructions," Elizabeth ordered.

"Now wait just a minute." Charlie stood up from his chair, kicking it behind him. The chair skidded and cracked against the wall. "None of that is necessary. Maddie is a valued member of the ISC."

"What happens to her, or anyone under *my* command for that matter, is none of your concern anymore."

The new Commander pressed the comm on her desk and requested assistance. Two armed security officers stood on both sides of Maddie, ready to carry out the orders. The agent who had been packing up Charlie's things stood at his side, grabbing him by the arm.

"No, wait, you can't do that!" Maddie insisted.

"Yes, I can. And, yes, I did," Elizabeth stated, folding her arms over her chest. "Please see she gets put into her dorm and this man is escorted out."

She nodded toward the security officers, who grabbed Maddie by both arms and pulled her out of the office. Charlie hollered but was dragged out of his former office.

"John!" Maddie cried out helplessly.

"Maddie!" John reached out for her. Two additional security guards stepped up, keeping him from making contact.

She could hear an argument ensuing between the siblings and her assistant, but she was too far away now to make out their words.

CHAPTER THREE

The guards shoved Maddie into a dorm room, and the door closed and locked quickly behind her. She started banging her fists and kicking the door, but no one came. Once she wore herself out without getting a response, she turned and sat on the bed. She scanned the room quickly, realizing where she was.

"I'm in my old quarters."

She was back in the same room that she was placed in when she first came to the agency two years ago. The walls were still barren, and it still had the same colorless hotel room feeling to it. Maddie grumbled and lay face down on the bed.

What a day this turned out to be! Finding out there had been the mistake in the lab which resulted in the switch between her and Mack, and now this. She wasn't even allowed back in her apartment. Maddie felt her entire world had turned upside down.

After a while, she jumped up from the bed and began to pace. She had lost track of time and felt like she was going to lose her mind. A knock on the door caused her to jump.

"Maddie." John rushed over to her.

She threw her arms around him, holding him tightly to her. His heart pounded was in his muscular chest as they embraced.

"What's going on?" she asked.

John eventually broke his hold, grabbed her by the hands, and led her back to the bed.

"Charlie has been escorted out of the ISC. Elizabeth has taken over. The official statement is the governing agency which presides over the ISC has deemed his recent decision-making unfit for command. You have been removed from active duty and will be kept in here until further notice."

"I can't go to our home?"

"Our marriage isn't being recognized, Maddie." He gently stroked her cheek. "I've tried arguing but all it did was demote me to mess hall clean up duty for a week. I'm revoked from flying in any off-world missions in the interim."

"What does she mean by recent decision-making? Namely me?"

John hesitated. "Partly. Apparently, he was able to justify you to the higher ups. It was the pregnancy that tipped the scales."

Maddie closed her eyes. She had wondered if there would be any backlash on Charlie for letting their son be raised by their clones. It was the hardest decision she had ever had to make but their son was better off. At least that's what she kept telling herself. The life Maddie and John had chosen was dangerous, and she could never live with herself if anything were to happen to Lucas.

"We gave up Lucas. On Charlie's orders," Maddie said.

"I know."

"That wasn't good enough?"

"It's apparently a lot of things, Maddie. That was just one of many things Elizabeth said."

If Elizabeth had been in the room, Maddie would have knocked out the woman. She couldn't remember ever feeling this mad before.

"Where does she get off? Who the hell does she think she is?" Maddie ranted.

"Our new commander," John gently said.

"And, what, you are okay with this?" Maddie demanded.

"No, of course not. This has been quite a shock to me as well. There just isn't a point in yelling about it. That won't change anything."

John looked warily at her. Today had been hard on both of them. She laid her head on his chest, cradled under his chin.

"It has been a long time since I've been afraid of losing you," he said.

"I'm not going anywhere," she promised.

His arms shook in fear as his hands rubbed her back.

"I'm afraid if I let you go, you'll disappear."

"John." Maddie looked up into his blue eyes, watching the mixture of love, fear, and pain rage in his eyes. "I love you. Regardless of everything going on around us, that will never change."

"Oh, Maddie, I love you." His lips lightly brushed against hers.

"Anything else going on I should know?" Maddie was almost afraid to ask.

"Hunter is going out of his mind in the lab. He's been helping Dr. Brody give Elizabeth the evidence to support our most recent discovery. Mack has been pretty much in the dark about it. She just knows that you are here. Naturally, Elizabeth refused Mack's request to see you when she gets back."

"Gets back?"

"Mack is out running maneuvers with Seth and Jackson on the new flight systems you designed in the *Black Rose*."

"What's going to happen?" she asked, unable to keep her voice from shaking.

"I wish I knew. It's been a long time since I've been scared of losing you. I don't like this feeling."

She closed her eyes again, breathing in the fresh scent of rosewood and citrus from his aftershave. Slowly, she calmed down as she listened to the rhythm of his heartbeat.

The buzzing of her communicator cuff snapped them out of their momentary bliss. Elizabeth's voice ordered both of them to her office.

"I guess now is as good of a time as any to find out," John said, kissing her forehead.

#

John and Maddie joined hands as they walked into Elizabeth's office. Maddie was surprised how quickly the woman transformed the space. It no longer resembled the office of Charlie Westlake. Brightly colored paintings decorated the walls, along with numerous diplomas. Several plants hung from the ceiling. Even though the facility appeared warm and inviting, Maddie felt uncomfortable.

"Please, have a seat." Elizabeth motioned to two brand new leather chairs.

"Thank you," Maddie said.

"I've had a long talk with Dr. Brody. Your assistant is filling an official report to Washington with the findings. I will need to see all the proof before any formal announcement can be made."

"Proof?" Maddie questioned.

"Of your legitimacy. Of course, there is still the matter of the clone, regardless of which one of you it is."

Maddie's eyes narrowed at the other woman who stared at her expressionless.

"What do you have against clones?" Maddie asked.

"I have nothing against clones. They serve their purpose," she flatly said.

"You talk as if clones aren't human beings," John stated.

"Of course they are human beings. They are people created in a lab whose sole purpose is to keep the secret of the ISC and our allies. Or have you forgotten that?"

"Of course not. My clone is raising my son to protect him," John snapped back.

"Hmm." Elizabeth pressed her lips together in disapproval. "Regardless, as I've said, the matter will be delicately looked into."

"Elizabeth, forgive me --" Maddie began.

"Commander Levette," Elizabeth sharply corrected her.

"My apologies, Commander, but what is to happen to me now?" Maddie asked.

"Dr. Brody has already given me enough evidence to support your earlier claim. It seems I owe you an apology. My earlier behavior was unprofessional of me, and I apologize," Elizabeth stated.

There was still no warmth or feeling in the woman's voice. Maddie felt like she wanted to tell the other woman where she could stick her apology, but ultimately knew enough to play along.

"Apology accepted." Maddie nodded.

"Now, that being said, you've been reevaluated and have been reinstated in the lab but not on the field," Elizabeth informed her.

"Why is that?"

"Because I am going to need you in the lab working with Dr. Brody and his team to make sure this mistake can never happen again. You are a valuable member of this organization, Agent Brooks."

Maddie raised an eyebrow. *So it's Agent Brooks now?*

"It's a pity we've only scratched the surface of your potential. The question is what do we do with the clone now?" Elizabeth questioned, almost absentmindedly.

"Her name is Mack." Maddie narrowed her eyes.

"The problem we are facing is there are technically three Madison Rhodes." Elizabeth ignored Maddie's statement.

"Mack has been a trusted professional for the ISC for the last seven years. You can't cast her aside now. What do you plan on doing?"

"That matter is still under investigation," Elizabeth informed them.

Elizabeth's business-like tone was beginning to grate on Maddie. She was talking about Mack as if she wasn't a person.

"Under investigation? You've got to be kidding me." Maddie threw her hands up in exasperation.

"In the meantime, I think it would be best if she hears the news coming from you rather than me," Elizabeth said.

"The news?" Maddie asked.

"Yes. That Ms. Rhodes is a clone." Elizabeth looked surprised and slightly aggravated that Maddie would question her.

"Absolutely not." John shook his head. "Besides, I thought you were waiting to hear back from Washington?"

"I'm waiting to hear back from them regarding what to do with her. She still ought to know before she gets blind-sided."

"You can't tell her. Trust me, I know. The news she is actually the clone, not me, will devastate her," Maddie informed her.

"You seemed to come to terms without any issues," Elizabeth pointed out.

That did take a little wind out of Maddie's sails. She faltered for a second before she regained her train of thought.

"I had no choice in the matter. People's lives were in danger. We were constantly under attack during that time. Mack doesn't pose a danger. She's a squad leader, for crying out loud. No, this is an entirely different situation than we were in two years ago. The information that Mack is a clone and not me should only stay in this office," Maddie insisted.

"That I'm a what?" the question came from behind them.

Maddie's heart skipped a beat. For a second, she closed her eyes before turning around. Mack leaned against the back of the door, still wearing her flight jacket. No one had heard her enter the office. Color had drained from her face and she had to use the door to hold herself up. John and Maddie exchanged a worried glance, not sure how to proceed.

"What were you saying, Maddie? That I'm a what? You think I'm a clone?" Mack asked.

"Mack, listen --" Maddie began.

"No, you listen." Mack snapped, pointing a finger in Elizabeth's direction. "I don't know who that woman is or why she is filling your head with lies, but there is no way that I'm your clone. There's just not."

"I'm afraid you are wrong." Elizabeth rose up from her chair, keeping her hands flat on her desk.

"Has this whole place gone mad? Charlie is gone, Maddie was locked up for twenty-four hours, and now you are saying this crap?" Mack fired back.

"Dr. Brody screwed up in the lab the day you were created. Maddie is not a clone. You are," Elizabeth's flat, emotionless voice informed her.

Mack paused, trying to collect herself. Maddie had to restrain herself to keep from jumping at the new commander. Her lack of sensitivity made Maddie's blood boil. *What happened to it being important that Maddie broke the news?*

"Maddie?" Mack asked, turning to her counterpart. The tearful look in her eyes tore at Maddie's heart.

"I'm so sorry, Mack."

"No," Mack argued.

"Mack ..." John started.

"No!" Mack yelled.

"I understand what you are feeling right now -- " Maddie began.

"You're right. You do. So you'll forgive me if I can't wrap my mind around this," Mack said.

Maddie took a step toward her, but Mack held up her hand.

"You come near me, and I'll punch you," Mack threatened.

"We can go to the lab and --" Maddie started.

"And what? Destroy me? Study me?"

"Talk to Dr. Brody. Let him explain."

"No, I don't think so," Mack said before she swung open the door and ran out.

"What are you waiting for? After her!" Elizabeth ordered.

Maddie ran out the door with John close on her heels. He contacted Jackson on his communicator cuff as they raced to find where Mack ran off to. They searched but could not find her.

"Track her down. I don't care what you have to do," Elizabeth ordered through Maddie's communicuff.

"I could use sensors, but Mack would have taken the communicuff off by now," Maddie said.

"Agent Brooks, tear this whole place a part if you have to. Just find her."

"Understood."

Jackson met up with them, looking completely bewildered. Maddie apologized, letting him know she would explain everything later after they found Mack. John contacted his brother, Seth, to assist in finding Mack. Quietly, the four teammates searched the agency but could not find a trace of her.

"Jackson, would Mack have a particular hiding place?" Seth questioned, running a hand through his blonde streak in his hair.

He had raven hair and as long as she had known him bleached a streak through a patch from root to tip. When she originally asked him about it, he said it was to help differentiate from Logan but even after his twin died, Seth kept bleaching the streak.

"Mack doesn't hide," Jackson said, shaking his head.

"Maddie, think. If this was you, where would you go?" John asked.

Maddie thought about it for a minute. She had a feeling that Mack left the agency undetected. If that was the case, she knew where Mack was.

"You guys stay here," Maddie instructed.

"No way, I'm going with you," Jackson protested.

"Jackson, I get it, believe me, but no. This is between Mack and myself," Maddie emphatically replied.

Jackson opened his mouth to argue with her but instead shrugged his shoulders. He knew that Maddie was right.

"Take care of her."

"You know I will."

#

Maddie left the agency and went to the same park where she had seen her other counterpart at earlier in the day. It was pouring rain so she knew the park would be deserted. By the time she got to the park, her clothes were soaked. She saw Mack on the swings, sticking her legs out in the air with very little force so she was barely moving.

"Hey," Maddie said, leaning against the post.

"Hey." Mack didn't look up at her.

Maddie watched as Mack slowly kicked her legs up, moving the swing only slightly.

"I'm not going to ask if you are okay."

"Good."

"Do you want to talk to Dr. Brody?"

"Eventually. I think I've already pieced together what happened. Computer program screwed up, gave the memories to the wrong girl. Wayne didn't want to own up to his mistake, so he tried to fix it. How far off the target am I?"

"Bull's-eye."

"Figured. Stupid, stupid, stupid," Mack muttered, still not meeting Maddie's gaze.

"How did you know about the computer program?" Maddie asked.

"Because it was the first thing I worked on after being fully welcomed into the agency," Mack informed her.

Mack started to swing herself a little higher.

"This doesn't have to change anything," Maddie said.

Mack jumped off the swing and landed gracefully on her feet. "Who are you kidding? It changes everything."

"No, Mack. Do you remember what you told me the day I was brought here? That I was flesh and blood. I was the same person I always was, this was just something new to add to that."

"That's bullshit," Mack spat out.

"So it's the truth when you said it, but it's bull when I do?"

"Yes," Mack quickly responded.

"No, it's not. It doesn't change everything you have done. The lives that you have saved. Nothing has come undone."

"Except for me."

"Mack --"

"How can you be so calm right now? How were you so calm then? I don't understand this," Mack frustration seeping in her voice.

"Because our biology, our makeup, who we are hasn't changed with this new bit of information. It's our perception that has."

"That perception is pretty fucking important," Mack cursed as she started pacing.

"Why is it so important?"

"Because I always thought I was better than you! All right? Are you happy now?" Mack stopped her pacing and yelled.

"Better than me?" Maddie was shocked by this admission.

"Yes. You were this skittish little creature, so meek and mild. I could hardly believe we shared the same DNA. I knew you wouldn't last out there on missions."

"But I did. I think I fared pretty well."

"You know what? You really did." Mack gave her a small smile. "I marveled at the way you handled yourself after you were brought here. I respected the way you kept yourself together when, Lord knows, everyone would have understood if you had fallen apart. You surprised us all, Maddie. But at the end of the day, I was still better than you."

Maddie picked up a slightly deflated basketball which had been left on the playground and rolled it around in her hands. Mack watched her for a moment before running a hand through her short, wet hair.

"We all expected you to crumble. Did you know that? We even had a medical room waiting for you in case you went into shock. But not you. After one night of crying, you were fine. Why is that? Huh?" Mack demanded as she began to pace once again.

"I don't know, Mack. Yes, it was upsetting. It flipped my entire world upside down. But I didn't feel like I could really fall apart. I was faced with a situation where enemies I didn't even know existed wanted me dead. If I didn't keep it together, I would be giving them opportunity to take me out."

"Yeah, I guess that's true," Mack slowly said, kicking a rock into a mud puddle.

"At the end of the day, you and I are different. Regardless of who was born and who was created in a lab, it's our experiences over the last seven years which made us different. You said it yourself."

"Yeah, we are different." Mack sighed. "So that's it, huh? That's the secret to your mental stability?"

"Truthfully? That, and the breakfast we had the first day I was there," Maddie answered.

"Breakfast?" Mack stopped her pacing.

"Yes, the first breakfast. The day I met the real John for the first time."

"Oh, good Lord." Mack shot Maddie a dirty look.

"It's true. I looked into his eyes and I knew that I was going to be okay. Something changed inside of me."

Mack rolled her eyes but then she softened. "I could almost physically see the bond between you two forming at the table. I pointed it out to Jackson. It didn't make any sense to me at the time. I worried slightly at first because I thought since you were my clone, if you had a crush on anyone, it would be Jackson. I was relieved when you fell for John. It doesn't change the fact I thought you were my clone. You were a copy of me. I was the standard for which you were compared to. You were just the kid sister trying to catch up. And now ..."

"Most of that is still true, Mack."

Maddie walked over to the other woman and stood face-to-face with her.

"Who you are hasn't changed, Mack. You are still the strong, independent woman that everyone loves and admires. I look up to you as if you are my big sister. You are still the measuring stick for me. I am still trying to keep up with you in the field. I don't know if I could have done some of the things you have."

"You don't understand. I've been living your life for the last seven years," Mack despondently said.

Without warning, Mack punched Maddie hard in the face, sending her counterpart to the ground. Water and mud splashed up when Maddie landed. She held her hand to her face, momentarily relieved when she didn't see blood. Anger replaced the relief as she looked at her counterpart. Maddie jumped up and ran at Mack, knocking the other woman down. They rolled around in the mud, punching and clawing at each other. Maddie made a conscious effort to only block Mack with her robotic right arm and punch with her human left. Eventually, Mack got the better of the exchange. She threw Maddie off of her, backing up to sit on the merry-go-round.

"Do you feel better now?" Maddie quizzed as she attempted to catch her breath.

"No, I don't." Mack looked down-trodden as she used her feet to push the merry-go-round.

Mack stopped moving the park equipment, covering her muddy face with her hands and began to cry. Maddie walked over to the merry-go-round and sat beside Mack. Mack looked over at her and grabbed her hand. Something was off when she looked at Maddie. She saw something flicker in her counterpart's eyes but, whatever it was, quickly dissipated.

"I've been living your life for the last seven years," Mack repeated.

"I lived your life, too," Maddie reminded her.

"Jackson ..." Mack's voice trailed off.

"Loves you, not me. Just like John loves me, not you."

"I know. Do you think this will change anything?"

"He's worried to death over you right now. Nothing is going to change the way that man feels about you."

"Are you sure?"

"I would bet my life on it."

"This explains something though."

"Explains what?"

"Why I miss home so much. I was supposed to be there."

Maddie slowly nodded, hiding the frown she felt. She had been conflicted when given the choice to go back home or to join the agency but didn't regret her decision. The only reason she occasionally checked in on the clone leading her former life was to look upon her son, Lucas.

"Do you regret it?" Mack asked. Maddie didn't need to get her to clarify the question.

"No. I'm happy here."

"And you're thriving. I've been so proud of you."

"Do you ... regret it?"

"If I'm being honest, sometimes I do. I'm happy with what I do. I wouldn't give up Jackson for anything. Sometimes ... sometimes I wonder if it wasn't for him, if I would have asked Charlie to let me go home by now."

"Charlie's not here anymore," Maddie reminded.

"I know. What's up with that?"

"Apparently there were some higher ups who disagreed with a few of his decisions."

Mack scoffed. "Blowhards. Who's the new girl? Do we know anything about her?"

"Her name is Elizabeth Levette," Maddie told her. "Apparently, she's John and Seth's sister."

"Elizabeth!" Mack exclaimed in surprise. "Wow, I wouldn't have guessed that Elizabeth Levette and their sister was one in the same."

"You've heard of her?" Maddie asked in shock.

"Oh, yeah. Charlie mentioned to me before if he had to retire, he thought she would take his place. I've heard a lot about her over the years. She's a tough cookie. Very by the book. Super business-like. Exactly what you would expect from a bureaucrat. It makes sense the higher ups would replace Charlie with someone like that. Still, John and Seth's long lost sister."

"It came as quite a shock to John. I'm not even sure if Seth knows yet."

"Wow. What a crazy day."

"Are you ready to go back yet, or do you want to roll around in the mud some more?"

The rain had washed most of the mud off their faces, but clumps of mud was still caked to their hair and clothing.

"Don't we look like a pair of water-logged rats?" Mack teased, smiling a little.

"There you are. I was wondering." Maddie smiled.

"You still need to work on your fighting. Hand-to-hand, I could take you," Mack teased.

"You can't judge me based on that. I wasn't trying to hurt you. Besides, I'm not as dominate with the left arm."

"You really should work on it. However, your punches have improved. Logan would have been proud."

The mere mention of John's other brother made Maddie's stomach turn into knots. Logan had given his life to save her and his twin brother, Seth. Maddie could never forget his sacrifice. She still felt guilty over his death.

"Come on. Let's go." Mack jumped up and held out her hand to Maddie.

"Are you sure you are okay?" Maddie asked, accepting Mack's hand.

"I reserve the right to freak out or break down at any time, but I'm okay right now," Mack answered honestly.

CHAPTER FOUR

"What the hell happened to you?" John asked as Maddie and Mack walked back into Elizabeth's office.

"Mud wrestling," Mack simply replied.

Elizabeth raised her perfectly plucked eyebrow over the women's appearances but didn't remark on it.

"Commander, I want to apologize for my behavior," Mack said. "My reaction was disrespectful, and I'm sorry. I was just … shocked."

"Understood." Elizabeth curtly nodded.

"How cool is it going to be with our baby sister running this joint?" Seth excitedly asked.

Elizabeth pressed her thin lips together. Apparently Seth and Elizabeth's reunion went as smoothly as hers and John's. Maddie knew Seth was trying to lighten up the mood, but Elizabeth did not seem to want to play along.

"This is not a happy family reunion. This is work. This is business. As far as I'm concerned, I don't have brothers," Elizabeth sternly informed them, tapping her finger on her desk.

She might as well have punched both of her brothers in the stomach. Pain reflected on both John and Seth's faces from her remark. Seth's shoulders slumped as he thrust his hands in his pockets. His normally brilliant green eyes were cloudy as her words hit their mark. Color drained from John's face as he rocked back on his heels. He looked down at the floor to avoid tearing up.

"Now if you'll excuse me, I have work to do. Dismissed," she ordered.

#

After both women had showered and gotten into clean clothes, the team regrouped in Maddie and John's living room.

"What do you think she is going to do?" Jackson asked.

"She pulled me off of duty initially, but she didn't say anything about Mack," Maddie said.

"I know. That's what is worrying me." Mack frowned.

"What if Elizabeth ordered to have Mack killed?" Jackson's voicewas drenched in worry.

"I don't think that's realistic." Maddie shook her head.

"Why? You've proved you two can touch without death. And we know now the other law isn't valid."

"You mean, if one dies, so does the other?"

Jackson nodded. "I mean, Logan's clone is still…"

His voice trailed off. Logan was still a touchy subject

among the team. The fact that Logan's clone was still living the life set up for him in Charleston was slightly comforting, but only marginally.

"Just because what we considered laws turned out to be fallible doesn't mean we know everything. We've only begun the investigation." Maddie looked down at the floor, unable to meet Jackson's eyes.

The team fell into silence, still considering what Maddie had said. She had only scratched the surface with her cloning project. There were still many questions they had which she hadn't been able to answer yet. The news there had been a mistake made previously threw all her current research out the window.

"Regardless of what happens, we are family. We stick together," Maddie told Mack, grabbing her hand.

Mack gave her a grateful smile and a small squeeze.

#

All off-world missions had been suspended for two weeks while Elizabeth organized her command and settled in. Mack seemed fine during that time. She even began to relax a little, which made Maddie breathe a little easier. Still, Maddie kept a close eye on her counterpart.

Elizabeth refused anyone who requested to see her, and no communication had been passed down. Most of the teams started to get a little antsy to get back to the day-to-day business. Several of them threw themselves into heavier training. Some started to get more into recreational fun that was available, such as the paintball field or bowling.

Maddie and Hunter kept busy in her lab on one of their many projects. Mack retreated to her office, telling Maddie she was going to be working on plans for a new ship. Maddie hoped as long as Mack kept busy, she would be fine. It seemed like a great plan. At least, that's what Maddie thought.

"Maddie! They locked her up!" Jackson exclaimed, bursting into Maddie's office.

"Who?" Maddie questioned.

"Mack! She flipped out, started throwing things and broke Nick Kicker's nose."

"She broke Nick's nose?" Hunter asked.

"Poor kid." Jackson shook his head. "He was just trying to help."

"What happened?" Maddie asked.

"I don't know. I wasn't there. Will said he heard noises coming from her office. When he went in to check on her, she threw a paperweight at him. He said the office was pretty trashed so he went to get help. He met up with Nick in the hallway and they tried to calm her down. Nick grabbed her arm and she punched his nose in before Will was able to sedate her. Elizabeth has her secured in a dorm."

Maddie stood up and followed Jackson to where Mack was detained. Two armed security guards stood at the door.

"Is she awake?" Maddie asked.

"Oh, yeah. She's awake. Mad as a rattlesnake, too," the guard, Steven, stated.

"Let me in," Maddie commanded, placing her hands on her hips.

"I'm sorry, Commander Levette's orders," Steven replied.

"I can calm her down," Maddie said.

"Orders are orders," the other guard, Evan, spoke up.

"I will handle Commander Levette. Open the door."

"If she asks, just tell her Maddie knocked you out with her right arm. She'll believe you," Jackson said, a smile tugging at the corner of his mouth.

When both men looked unmoved by Jackson's light-hearted tease, he elbowed her. Maddie sighed and rolled up the sleeve on her right arm and pulled down on the synthetic material which made up the fake skin, exposing the mechanical arm. Steven and Evan's eyes widened as they stared before exchanging glances and stepping aside.

"Really? You had to make a robotic arm comment?" Maddie raised an eyebrow.

"Hey, it got us in, didn't it?" Jackson questioned as he opened the door.

Cautiously, Jackson and Maddie stepped inside. Broken glass from the TV littered the floor.

Maddie sidestepped the pieces of a broken lamp. Two chairs were turned over by a little table. Mack had pulled the comforter off the bed and judging by the cuts in the fabric had unsuccessfully attempted to rip apart the mattress. A glass whizzed by Maddie's head, smashing against the wall.

"Oh, what, are you two here to tranquilize me again?" Mack demanded as they stepped into the center of the room.

"What? No, don't be ridiculous," Maddie replied.

"Commander Levette doesn't know that we are here," Jackson said.

"Oh, yes, she does. She's been watching me on camera."

She turned to face a far corner of the room where a video camera was perched. The red light was on. They were, indeed, being watched.

"Probably just trying to figure out how crazy I am!" Mack yelled at the camera.

"Just calm down, all right? Talk to us," Maddie encouraged.

Mack paced feverishly in the room, muttering under her breath.

"You *are* acting like a crazy person. Keep this up, and you will be sedated again," Maddie cautioned.

"Sedate me, then! I don't give a shit, Maddie!" Mack screamed, still keeping her paces.

"Stop it!" Maddie yelled, grabbing Mack by the shoulders and halting her strides.

Mack let out a loud, exasperated breath, but wouldn't meet Maddie's eyes. After a moment, she smacked Maddie's hands away from her shoulders and turned away from both of them. Jackson stepped beside her, placing his hand lightly on the small of her back. She leaned into him after a moment, resting her head on his shoulder.

"Please talk to me," Jackson begged. "I love you, Mackenzie. Don't push me away."

"Jackson, I love you, too."

"I really want to be here for you but I can't if you don't let me in."

"Are you sure you want to know?"

"Of course I do. We're partners. No matter what's going on. What happened?" Jackson asked.

"Nothing happened."

"Don't do that. Don't shut us out," Maddie pleaded.

"No, that's just it. Nothing happened. I was sitting at my desk, working on a new schematic for an engine, when it occurred to me." Mack pulled away from Jackson and kept her back to them.

"What?" Maddie asked.

"That you were right."

Maddie and Jackson exchanged looks, completely confused.

"You are going to have to do a little better than that. I'm right all the time," Maddie attempted to joke.

"Two years ago, when you were brought to the ISC. I kept the information from you that I had requested a new clone to be created."

"I remember."

"You got mad at Charlie when he told you, telling him that he couldn't play God with people," Mack reminded her.

"I remember that, too."

"You came to me after speaking with Charlie."

"I did. I felt like Charlie believed that clones were disposable."

"I defended Charlie and the creation of the second clone. I still stand by that decision, by the way."

"I never second guessed you."

"I thought you were being overly sensitive. But now, I think you were right," Mack softly said.

"Honey --" Jackson began, reaching for her.

"No!" Mack shouted, stomping her foot, but still keeping her back to them.

The forcefulness behind Mack's reaction took Maddie by surprise. She glanced over at Jackson who stared agape at her. He was just as surprised as she was.

"No! I will not be silenced! They don't care! All they care about is their precious secret. Do you think Charlie gave it a second thought when I asked for the other clone to be created? No! Two weeks later, poof!" She waved her hands wildly as she spun around, her dark blue eyes looking unfocused. "Another Madison! Blissful and happy. And then suddenly with a child that wasn't technically hers. More manipulation on behalf of the ISC and Dr. Wayne Brody."

"Mack …"

"That woman's entire life was fabricated, same as mine, only she has no idea of the war which we constantly fight. No concept of the truth behind her existence."

Maddie tried to come up with a counter-argument but couldn't. She stood back, letting her friend rant.

"Do you think Elizabeth Levette gives a damn about me? Do you think she would lose a second of sleep if she ordered my death tonight?"

"Yes, I do."

"You do?" Mack raised her eyebrow, chewing on her bottom lip. "Oh, right, because you believe the best in people. Grow up, Maddie. If she doesn't give a shit about her own flesh and blood, what makes you think she would hesitate before giving the order to end my life? That bitter little woman," she snarled.

Maddie had never seen Mack's temperament change as fast as it had. One minute she was calm, the next she was screaming at the camera on the wall. Maddie had also never heard her curse as much as she did.

"You know what the kicker is?" Mack quizzed, laughing manically. "If Elizabeth wanted to, she could make me forget that I know I'm the clone! How simple would that be? I would just go to sleep and forget this day even happened."

Mack dropped to her knees and covered her face in her hands. Her whole body shook as she cried. Jackson got down on his knees in front of her, wrapping his arms around Mack's shoulders. Mack leaned into him, burying her face into his dark hair. It broke Maddie's heart as she watched the couple, unsure what she should do.

The two security guards, Steven and Evan, entered the room, brushing Maddie aside. Steven grabbed Jackson by the arm and attempted to pull him to his feet, but Jackson shoved him off.

"Get the hell out of here!"

Maddie gasped as Steven swung at Jackson, but he blocked the punch and landed one of his own. Blood started to trickle out of the corner of Steven's mouth. He wiped the blood on his sleeve and charged Jackson. The two men fell over a broken chair as they fought each other.

Maddie looked over at Mack but she was staring off into space. She didn't seem to notice the altercation.

"Cut it out!" Maddie cried out, attempting to pull Jackson off of Steven.

The guard's face was bloodied from his mouth and nose, bruising beginning to form around his eye. Maddie managed to separate the two, keeping a firm hold on the collar of Jackson's shirt.

During the melee, Evan stuck a needle in Mack's arm, and she slumped into Evan's arms.

"Where are you taking my wife?" Jackson demanded as Evan scooped Mack up into his arms.

"She'll be safe. She's going under medical care," Evan gently replied.

"No, wait, you can't do this!" Maddie insisted, pulling on Steven's arm.

"Commander Levette's orders," Steven informed them, jerking away from her. He winced as his left eye started to puff up. "And I'll be filing a report on you, Gray."

"Be my guest," Jackson said through gritted teeth.

#

The door to Elizabeth's office slammed against the wall as Jackson stormed in ahead of Maddie. He tossed papers off of the desk, leaning in Elizabeth's face.

"What have you done with my wife?" Spit dripped from the corner of his mouth as his fist pounded the desk.

"Jackson!" Maddie pulled at his arm.

Elizabeth looked completely unfazed at Jackson, leaning back in her chair and taking a sip from the tea cup she had been holding.

"You can't wipe her memory! You can't do that to her!"

"Actually, I can," Elizabeth casually said, taking off her reading glasses and tossed it on the desk next to Jackson's hand. He snatched the tea cup from her hands and threw it against a wall, shattering against a bookshelf. "Agent Gray, I have no intentions of performing any kind of procedure on the clone."

"Oh, thank God." Maddie slipped down into a chair, looking relieved.

"What are you doing to her?" Jackson asked.

"Agent Gray, I'm not going to harm her. I am not your enemy here," the Commander replied.

Maddie and Jackson both took a deep breath, trying to get their emotions back under control. His body shook as he reigned in his anger, slowly backing up from the desk.

"I'm sorry. You are right. She ... she's my wife. She's my entire world. I'm sorry."

For the first time, Maddie saw Elizabeth soften. Her eyes shown a warmth Maddie hadn't seen before as her face relaxed.

"It's okay. I understand, Jackson. Mack is going to be sedated for a little while, just to help calm her down. Then we will work on getting her mentally healthy."

"So, you aren't going to wipe her memory?" Maddie asked.

"I could. Might be better for Mack if I did. But I would prefer that her brain isn't manipulated any further, wouldn't you?" Elizabeth kindly asked.

"Absolutely," Maddie agreed.

"Excellent. She can still be saved."

"Saved? So you are interested in helping her?" Maddie asked.

"Of course. I have no plans on destroying her. She's still invaluable to this organization. A brilliant mind, one of the top squad leaders we have, plus one of the best pilots I have ever seen."

Maddie pressed her lips together, her arms folding over her chest.

"You disagree with my assessment?" Elizabeth asked, raising an eyebrow.

"Not at all. Your analysis of Mack is spot on. I'm just wondering why you didn't act this way toward me."

Elizabeth's eyes flashed in anger for a second before regaining her composure. "What do you mean?"

"When you thought I was a clone. You told me that you wouldn't recognize my marriage to your brother and clones don't belong within the walls of the ISC. I was then locked away until I could be … what was the word? Oh, right. Re-evaluated."

Elizabeth gave her a humorless smile. "What's your point?"

"I'm just wondering what the difference is in your eyes between myself and Mack? Have I not proven myself invaluable to the ISC? Do I not share the same brilliant mind as my counterpart? Or am I less valuable because I never learned how to fly?"

"Mack has years of training and missions under her belt. As a soldier and squad leader, she has more than paid back the cost of her development."

"Her development? You mean genetic manipulation?" Maddie fired back.

"Maddie ..." Jackson tried to reach for her but she brushed him away.

"That's it, isn't it? When Dr. Brody tried to 'fix' his little gaffe and did these so-called enhancements to her. That's the difference, isn't it?"

"That's part of it," Elizabeth calmly said. "Another part is that she has saved lives, whereas you've been the cause of many deaths, including my brother."

The way Elizabeth spoke without any emotion regarding the death of Logan sent Maddie over the edge.

"Don't you *dare* speak about Logan! He was more my brother in those four months than he's ever been yours."

"That's enough!" Elizabeth snapped, slapping her desk.

Maddie clinched her mouth shut, her eyes narrowing across the desk. Elizabeth took a deep breath, releasing her frustration.

"I'm sorry," Elizabeth said, and edge of contempt in her voice. "Mack is going to remain under medical care, and I have high hopes that she'll be able to become the woman that you all know once again. Unless either of you disagree with my course of action?"

Jackson and Maddie both shook their heads.

"Good. I'm glad we are in agreement," Elizabeth nodded, dismissing them.

CHAPTER FIVE

True to Elizabeth's word, Mack was placed under medical care and wasn't allowed to have any visitors. Jackson was out of his mind with worry, to the point where John and Seth had to take him out to the paintball field to get his mind off of things.

To everyone's surprise, Elizabeth summoned Maddie to her office a few days later with instructions for Maddie to come alone.

"How's Mack?" Maddie asked, taking a seat in one of the leather office chairs.

"Not looking too good at the moment. Whenever we bring her out of sedation, she starts yelling again. I'm hoping that she will learn that as long as she is calm and rational, she won't be put back under," Elizabeth told her.

"I want to thank you for not wiping her memory," Maddie said.

"You are welcome. I just hope she snaps out of this soon, or the higher ups may make me."

"Who are the higher ups?"

"The Pentagon."

"Oh, right," Maddie bashfully said, blood flooding her cheeks. She should've known that.

"I've been watching you these last few days."

"I figured as much." Maddie felt her cheeks redden as she looked at the floor.

"You really are an intriguing person. I can see why Commander Westlake was so protective of you."

"Protective?" Maddie looked up, leaning her head to the side.

"Very much so. I used to read his reports when I worked in Washington. He always spoke highly of you."

"Wow, I didn't know," Maddie said, slightly taken aback. She always considered him to be closer to Mack than her. "With all the commotion, I didn't get a chance to say goodbye."

"He understands."

"Is this what you wanted to see me about?" Maddie asked.

Elizabeth paused, as if still considering something.

"Would you like to grab a cup of coffee with me?" Elizabeth asked.

"Uh, sure." Maddie didn't hide her surprise. This was a highly unusual request.

"Off-campus."

"Oh, sure. Let me just let John know," Maddie said, chewing on the inside of her cheek as she reached for her wrist communicator.

"I'd rather that you didn't." Elizabeth stopped her.

"Pardon?" Maddie questioned.

"Leave your communicator cuff here as well," she instructed.

This was highly unusual and outside of protocol. Elizabeth didn't seem like the type that would randomly break the rules so whatever she wanted to speak with Maddie about, it had to be important. Maddie slipped her cuff off and placed it on Elizabeth's desk. For a moment, Maddie fidgeted as she pondered the other woman's intentions. She was momentarily grateful for the gun strapped to her ankle. If the new commander had changed her mind and decided to kill her away from the agency, she would be prepared. The two women walked in silence to a small cafe not too far from the agency.

#

"You can relax, Maddie. You aren't in trouble. Right now, don't think of me as your new commander. We're just two women having coffee."

Even with Elizabeth's reassurance, Maddie still felt uncomfortable. It had been awhile since she'd been out in public, away from the ISC. She hadn't made up her mind as to whether Elizabeth's intentions were good or not.

"I want you to know I've read your file. You've had an interesting couple of years with the ISC," Elizabeth noted as they sat down.

"Yeah, interesting isn't quite the word for it, but thank you," Maddie dryly said.

Maddie started chewing on the inside of her cheek, feeling nervous about being out with her new commanding officer. She put in her order for coffee, silently wishing they were having this meeting back in Elizabeth's office.

"I can't tell you how many times I've read your account of the Mihun posing as Commander Westlake. Your actions were nothing short of heroic," Elizabeth said, breaking into her thoughts.

"Heroic?" Maddie felt skeptical. Elizabeth was talking about it as if it was something for her to be proud of. "You mean, being kidnapped, having my right arm removed, and watching many people die?"

Maddie wanted to add *including your brother* but quickly decided against it.

There was an uncomfortable pause as the waitress came with their coffees.

"No one else picked up on the fact it was an impostor. Everyone was fooled. If it wasn't for you, we would've known too late and the Earth, along with countless other worlds, could have been destroyed."

"It's good that's the picture you paint." Maddie stared down into her coffee cup.

"What's the picture in your head?" Elizabeth asked, tilting her head to the side.

"I see the look on John's face as he was tied to a chair and I was overpowered. I feel the gun being pointed to my head, being forced to my knees. The moment when I thought I was going to die."

"But you didn't," Elizabeth pointed out.

"Thanks to Mack."

"You really are highly unusual," Elizabeth muttered, pouring sugar into her cup.

"What's so weird about me?" Maddie asked, slightly bewildered.

"How quick you are to give Mack credit."

"I don't see how that is unusual. She did save my life."

"I'm not discounting that, Maddie. Your file ... is very interesting."

"Tell me what's so interesting." Maddie raised an eyebrow as she stirred cream into her coffee.

"You prefer a lab, but you do excel in the field. You are strong and brave, but you would rather let Mack take the lead."

"I still fail to see what's unusual about me," Maddie commented.

"I think you forget how unusual your situation is to begin with. Not only do you know your clone, but you are friends with her. Yet, you two act like siblings."

"Mirror images," Maddie said with a sly smile. "May I ask you a question?"

"Of course."

"Do you have a clone?"

"No." Elizabeth shook her head. "It wasn't necessary for me."

"What makes you say that?"

"I don't go off-world so I'm not in any real danger. I get to communicate with my adoptive mother weekly as my position currently stands.

Besides," the spoon hit the side of the cup as she looked down. "… no one would miss me if something were to happen."

"John and Seth would."

"We're not discussing them."

"I'm sorry if I overstepped my bounds."

"You didn't." Elizabeth sighed. She shifted uncomfortably in her chair, looking desperate to change the subject. "I am beginning to understand now why Charlie took the direction he did when it came down to the two of you. Is that why you took on the cloning program?"

"A little. I wanted to try to understand it better. Try to improve the program, maybe. See what direction the commission wants to go in next and lead it there."

"Admirable."

"Thanks. Is that why you asked me out for coffee?"

"So quick to jump to the chase." Elizabeth gave her a small smile.

"I'm sorry. I'm just a little out of my element here," Maddie said, her voice shaking slightly from being a little nervous. "I figured it was either that, or you wanted to kill me."

The new commander took a long sip from her cup and then brushed back her jet black hair.

"I have no intention on killing you Madison. Quite the opposite."

"Oh." She bit her lip.

"I … Hell, I'll just come out and say it. I've denied John and Seth's requests to see me," she said in a voice softer than Maddie had ever heard from her before.

So that's what this is about, Maddie thought.

"I heard. You can't ignore them forever," Maddie casually said.

"I used to work with the different alien technologies in the Pentagon. Whenever something new was discovered, my department was the one that signed off on it. Eventually, I moved up in the administration due to my high regard for rules and procedures and attention to details. I was the first they approached to take over the ISC. I took this post because of my brothers. But when I got here, I just got so ..."

"Angry?" Maddie finished.

"Yes!" Elizabeth exclaimed.

Several patrons of the cafe turned to stare at the two women. Elizabeth turned crimson under their gaze. Maddie quickly apologized to the strangers.

"I can understand that. I know John does. He's been there. Seth ... I'm not sure if he's as understanding."

"Can you tell me about them?" Elizabeth asked.

"Wouldn't it be better if you just got to know them?"

"I'm not sure if I'm ready for that yet," Elizabeth responded truthfully.

"I get it. John told me about your early childhood."

"Or lack thereof," Elizabeth dryly said.

Maddie nodded, running the tip of her finger around the rim of the coffee cup.

"I know how bad it tore him apart when he was separated from his siblings. It brought him down a dark path that only cleared up when Charlie found him. He took some of that anger out on Seth and Logan when they reconnected."

"I've read his files. He actually broke his hand punching Seth when he first came to the agency." Elizabeth looked like she was fighting a smile.

Maddie chuckled. "That's my guy."

"His files indicate a big change in his demeanor really started a little over two years ago," Elizabeth said with a little twinkle in her eye.

Maddie blushed slightly. "I've been told that."

"I'm glad to hear it. I'm glad to see it, too, actually. Unless you are focused on something, you two always look like you could rip each other's clothes off at any minute. I could use a little less of that." Elizabeth's tone bordered on teasing.

Maddie's blush grew crimson. "I'm sorry."

"I'm just a lonely, bitter woman who is jealous of the way you two can love." Elizabeth waved it off.

"Tell me about your life," Maddie encouraged.

Elizabeth looked at her skeptically over the brim of her coffee cup.

"You are my sister-in-law, after all." Maddie prodded. "You said it yourself. We're just two women out enjoying some fresh coffee. I'm interested,

Elizabeth. Tell me about yourself, and I'll tell you about your brothers."

"An exchange? All right. After I was taken away from my brothers, I was placed in a foster home. I got lucky. I was placed in a loving home with a wonderful, childless couple. The Dawsons were incredible to me. But, unfortunately, they were killed in a car accident after two years with them. I was heartbroken. I was placed in an orphanage where I was adopted by Donna Levette. She showed me a world I had never seen before. We moved from Ohio to Connecticut, where I went to the finest private schools and then to Stanford. I never wanted for anything."

"Ah, so you're spoiled. That explains a lot," Maddie teased.

Elizabeth grinned. "You can say that. But I worked hard to get where I am. No one handed me anything."

"I think that's a family trait."

Maddie noticed for the first time how pretty her commander was. When Elizabeth relaxed, she resembled Seth quite a bit. Her long, black hair framed her oval face nicely. It was the eyes that Maddie noticed more. It was the same shade of emerald that Logan and Seth shared. Now that she was away from the office, Elizabeth had the same gleam in hers that Maddie regularly saw in Seth's.

"All right, I spilled. So tell me about my brothers."

Elizabeth looked like she was anxious and slightly nervous. For a brief moment, Maddie contemplated teasing her, but decided to speak openly.

"It could be a social experiment, watching them. Each of them grew up differently, and it shows. You can see it to this day in the way they act. Seth is very jovial. He's so goofy and open. He seems to find the best in every person and every situation. He always looks for ways to break tension. He's one of my best friends. I always know I can trust and rely on him, no matter what's going on.John can have a temper but he's better at controlling it now. He's actually a fantastic artist. He draws things he's been a part of and occasionally dreams. His art is really … powerful. Now Logan," Maddie paused. "Logan was amazing. He was one hell of a fighter. He put all his frustrations into his training, into any mission he was a part of. He was closed off, had a lot of barriers up, but I was lucky enough to see him smile."

"Wow." Elizabeth leaned back in her chair."You speak of him with such reverence."

"Logan and Seth became brothers to me when I was first brought in. He gave up his life for me. I can never repay his sacrifice," Maddie softly said.

A single tear rolled down her face and into her coffee. They fell silent for a moment, tension between them palpable.

"I'm sorry, Maddie. Logan's death was one of the reasons I reacted to you the way I did during that first meeting," Elizabeth admitted.

"I can certainly understand that." Maddie wiped away a fresh tear. "I've read the multiple reports from Seth and watched what was left of the security footage. Logan didn't have to do what he did. There might have been a chance the three of us could have escaped. Or all three of us could have been killed. I wonder sometimes what went through his mind when he chose his path. He didn't make his decision lightly. I only had four months with him, but I loved him dearly. Now I strive to make sure his efforts weren't in vain."

"I can respect that. Thank you for your honesty."

Elizabeth unexpectedly reached across the table and grabbed Maddie's hand. She gave her an affectionate squeeze before letting go. She emptied her coffee cup, circling the rim with her finger.

"What is with Seth's bleach streak? He looks like a drunk skunk."

Maddie burst out laughing, spraying coffee across the table. Elizabeth grimaced as she handed Maddie some napkins to wipe the table up.

"I'm sorry."

"No, I suppose that's my fault for blurting out the question the way I did." Elizabeth wiped her face.

"I don't know. He really loves that streak. Often when he's nervous or annoyed, he tosses it over his shoulder." Maddie grinned. "It's actually ways I can tell if he's bluffing when we play poker. He just doesn't know I know it."

"I'm jealous you know him so well."

"We're family." Maddie shrugged. "Anything else you want to ask?"

"I'm not sure if I'm ready yet. But thank you."

"Anytime." Maddie gave her a warm smile.

"I had to get you away from the agency to really get to know you. I'm glad I did. But you know as soon as we get back --"

"I know, I know. Business as usual."

#

Mack came out of sedation the next day. This time, instead of the usual yelling, Mack went mute. She was despondent. The medical team had her placed on an IV since she refused to eat or drink anything. She moved very little and would stared off into space, never acknowledging anyone's presence. Maddie and Jackson sat by Mack's bedside, praying that the woman would turn her head or say something.

"I've never seen her like this." Worry broke through Jackson's voice.

"I have. This is very similar to how she was after Megan Gatewood's assault on you." Maddie gently patted him on the arm.

"She won't even look at me, Maddie. I don't like talking about her like this, not with her here."

"I don't think she is, Jackson. I'm not a head doctor, but I don't think she's with us."

"I don't know what to do. I've never not been able to reach her before. There's nothing medically wrong with her. But she...she just lies there."

Maddie studied Mack as she lay in the hospital bed, staring up at the ceiling. A part of her wanted to say that Mack was reacting like ... well, like she was told a clone would. Instead, she chose a different approach. She leaned over and brushed a few stray hairs from Mack's forehead.

"She's lost her purpose."

"Lost her purpose?" Jackson shook his head. "I don't understand."

"When Mack found out the truth, something changed within her."

Maddie had seen it in her eyes when they were on the playground and again when she ranted in the dorm room.

"When you were told that you were a clone, you didn't respond this way," Jackson commented.

"But you were prepared for me to react, weren't you?"

"Yes, actually. You surprised us."

"I still served a purpose, Jackson. I still felt like I had meaning, even if it was just keeping the secret of the ISC and keeping Mack alive. Mack and I can touch without death. There's another clone back home to protect the secret. Mack feels like she lost her purpose," Maddie tried to explain the best she could.

"She still has purpose here. If I could only reach her, I would tell her."

Jackson turned away from Maddie and stared down at the unresponsive Mack. He gently stroked her cheek, his eyes searching hers for a response. Mack did not turn her head.

"Come back to me, baby. I'm lost without you," Jackson whispered.

It broke Maddie's heart watching the pain that Jackson was going through. She racked her brain for something that would snap Mack out of her state, but nothing came to mind.

"She will," Maddie assured him. She wished she felt as confident as she sounded.

#

Two days went by and there was still no change in Mack. Maddie was shocked when she was summoned to one of the conference rooms and her team was there, including Mack. Her counterpart sat in a wheelchair, with an IV still in her arm. However, Maddie could not see any noticeable changes in her. She stared into the distance with a cold, blank look on her face.

"All right, I've got a mission for you," Elizabeth announced.

This news excited Maddie. Maybe this was exactly what Mack needed to snap out of it.

"What's going on?" Maddie asked.

"Are you familiar with a planet that we have dubbed PS-8755?" Elizabeth asked.

"I have. That's the Agonahan planet, right?" Jackson spoke up.

"It is. They need our help," Elizabeth stated.

She activated a projector, bringing up an image of a planet which looked remarkably similar to Earth up on the wall.

"What's going on ... Commander?" John asked, still unsure about addressing his sister with the title.

"PS-8755 is a planet rich with the mineral pluchiot which is a very rare mineral that, if utilized properly, can be very explosive. If concentrated correctly, it can blow a planet into space dust," Elizabeth explained.

"Wow," Maddie said in a low voice. Seth let out a low whistle, nodding in agreement.

"The Agonahans are the only race that can safely mine the mineral without risk of detonation. And they are being targeted," Elizabeth continued.

"By whom?" Seth asked.

"The Fabrega."

Maddie looked at her teammates for an explanation.

"Sorry, I keep forgetting that you don't know this stuff like Mack does. The Fabrega are a race of giants. They look almost like mythical ogres. The smallest of them is eight feet tall. They can get as tall as twenty feet. Normally, they keep to themselves," Seth explained.

"The Agonahans are the exact opposite in stature. They are roughly the size of an eight-year-old child," John stated.

"So the Fabrega want the pluchiot," Maddie said.

"They are ordering the Agonahans to surrender or they will enslave them. The Fabrega are not known for weapons manufacturing and can be incredibly clumsy. That leads me to believe maybe they are hired by someone else to extract the pluchiot," Elizabeth stated.

"So we are to go to PS-8755 to prevent a war," Jackson said.

"You five were requested by Rachel herself to come," Elizabeth nodded.

"Rachel?" Maddie questioned.

"Rachel?" Mack hoarsely asked.

Everyone was startled at hearing Mack's voice. The woman cleared her throat, attempting to talk again.

"The leader of the Agonahan people. Rachel requested us?" she wondered.

"Yes, she did. You were fundamental in negotiating the Agonahans' freedom from the Heamus clan several years ago. She's comfortable with you. Do you think you are good to go?" Elizabeth inquired.

"I'm ready." Mack's voice became more clear and steady. "How much time do we have?"

"It's a three day flight by way of our engines. Seth, I need you to get started on the system checks immediately," Elizabeth ordered.

"Right you are, Commander." Seth stood up and promptly left the room.

"What is it that we are looking at, exactly?" Mack asked.

Maddie let out a sigh of relief. Mack seemed to be returning to normal.

"Try to protect the Agonahans, see if you can't negotiate with the Fabrega. A large squadron will be heading to the planet a day after you so you have that time to prevent a war."

"Understood," Mack said.

She ripped the IV out of her arm and stood up. After a second, her knees buckled, and Jackson caught her before she hit the desk.

"Maybe I shouldn't have done that," Mack said, regaining her composure.

"Are you all right?" Maddie asked.

"I'm good. Let's do this."

As the team filed out of the conference room, Elizabeth grabbed Maddie's arm.

"Keep an eye out. If she starts acting crazy, take care of her. And take care of my brothers."

"I will," Maddie promised. "Are you going to talk to them?"

Elizabeth looked at her, still uncertain. "Take care of them," she repeated.

Mack had been medically cleared for the off-world mission by the time Seth had completed the system checks. Seth and Mack were already in the ship as Jackson, Maddie, and John piled in. Mack retreated to one of the sleeping quarters and would only come out when it was her shift to pilot the vessel. Even with Maddie's attempts to talk to Mack failing, the three day flight went by fast and before they knew it, they arrived at the planet.

CHAPTER SIX

Maddie had been to many worlds, but this one was the closest she had seen to Earth, only everything was miniature. All the houses, vegetation, and even the animal life were smaller. Seth had to land their ship in an open field because it was too large to fit in the Agonahan hangar. In the distance from the field was a tiny city bustling with small stores and businesses. Maddie could make out little vehicles that looked like something out of 1960s Earth only the vehicles hovered in the air, not touching the ground. One building taller than the others stood to the left of the field. Maddie assumed that one was the Agonahan government building. It looked like a large-scale construction was being built to its right.

"You look like an idiot with your mouth hanging open like that," Mack sharply said as she elbowed Maddie in the ribs.

Maddie frowned. Mack's mood hadn't improved much since they left Earth, but at least she was coherent.

A crowd of little people were heading their way. Leading the pack was a tiny woman with round, brown eyes and long, brown hair bound in a braid that she was practically walking on. The pack consisted of three men and another woman with long blonde hair in a braid. Mack got down on one knee to greet them.

"It's good to see you," the woman with the long brown hair greeted Mack warmly, hugging her.

The little woman practically squeaked when she talked.

"Rachel, I'm glad you called us." Mack returned the hug.

"It's been so long. I hate that it was under this condition." Rachel nodded. "I didn't know where else to turn."

"Let me introduce you to my team. My husband, Jackson." Mack motioned toward him.

Maddie and John exchanged looks. It was the first time either of them heard Mack introduce Jackson as her husband to anyone.

"It's an honor to meet you." Rachel smiled.

"And the rest of my team John, Maddie, and Seth," Mack introduced them in turn.

"A pleasure. This is my life partner, Samuel. The rest of my team Roger, Lawrence, and Zoe."

The teams shook each other's hands. Maddie marveled how tiny they were. At 5'5, she felt like a giant.

"I do apologize, but our new facilities are still under construction, as you can see," Rachel pointed over to the building to the right.

"It's quite all right. Will you be comfortable on our ship?" Mack asked.

"Yes, please," Rachel responded politely.

The two groups walked back on the large vessel and went into the meeting room area. The three men had to duck as they entered the conference area. Maddie felt like she was sitting at a kindergarten table. Her knees rested against the short table as she sat in the short yet sturdy chair.

"So what are we looking at, Rachel?" Mack asked.

"The Fabrega are after the pluchiot, as you know," Rachel stated.

"I've gotten the report." Mack nodded.

"They have given us four days to surrender or they will attack," Rachel stated in her high pitched voice.

"Are they open to negotiations?" Jackson asked.

Rachel looked almost startled that someone other than Mack spoke to her.

"Yes, but I fear even in negotiations, it will still cost my people everything," Rachel squeaked.

"I'm not going to let that happen." Mack's voice was smooth and steady.

Something in the way that Mack spoke made Maddie shiver. She felt there was still something wrong with Mack, even though she looked to be in complete control.

"Thank you, my friends." Rachel smiled at the team.

"Okay, so let's start with the negotiations," Maddie spoke up.

"Obviously." Mack rolled her eyes.

"What does that mean?" Maddie asked.

"Well, we wouldn't shoot first, then attempt to negotiate," Mack said, snarling.

"Of course not. I merely was opening up the discussion to see what Rachel was willing to negotiate for her people," Maddie stated.

"Why didn't you just ask her instead of saying something silly like that?" Mack asked.

"Where is this coming from?" Maddie inquired.

Mack didn't answer, just rolled her eyes again before giving her attention back to Rachel. Rachel looked confused and slightly embarrassed.

"I'm sorry. As I was saying," Maddie gave Mack a dirty look, which the other woman ignored, "what would you be willing to offer the Fabrega?"

"We will not part with the pluchiot. The mineral is far too dangerous in the wrong hands," Rachel stated.

"I agree," Mack said.

"But we do have some neuteroilum that we can offer," Samuel spoke up.

Maddie was taken aback by the high quality of Samuel's voice. She saw Seth out of the corner of her eye start to giggle. Maddie gave him a swift kick to shut him up.

"Forgive me for sounding ignorant, but what is neuteroilum?" Maddie asked.

"It is the oil that we use as an energy source. A little bit of neuteroilum lights our homes, cities, and even fuels our transportation. It does not break down and lasts for fifteen years before needing to refuel," Zoe explained, her voice just as high pitched as the others.

Zoe was smaller than the rest of her companions. As she spoke, her braid bounced against her back. Her wide brown eyes seemed a little too big for her sweet face.

"That sounds like a good place to start." Maddie smiled toward Zoe.

"Good. Then we are in agreement," Mack said, standing up from the table.

"Thank you all for coming," Rachel said.

The two groups shook hands before the Agonahans left the ship.

"I trust that you can draw up a proposal?" Mack asked Maddie.

"Yes, I can do that," Maddie said.

"Good. Glad to know that you have some purpose here." Mack's eyes narrowed.

Maddie had to cut her eyes away from the other woman to avoid the icy stare. *So she had been listening in the hospital bed.*

"Glad we understand each other. Jackson?"

Jackson scrambled up from the chair and followed Mack out of the room.

#

"What was all that about?" Seth asked.

"She's mad at me for some reason." Maddie frowned.

"What was that jab about you having purpose here?" John asked.

"When she crashed, Jackson and I were talking about it. I said that she had lost her purpose," Maddie explained.

"Ah, so she heard you," Seth said.

"I guess so." Maddie's frown deepened, her brows furrowing together.

"She's just angry at the whole situation," John said, gently rubbing her arm.

"And taking it out on me?" Maddie asked.

"It's easier for her to take it out on you," John noted, sympathetically.

"That's all well and good for her. But what happens when we get back home?" Maddie asked.

"Sis, no offense, but I don't think Mack is thinking about that," Seth gently said.

"Maybe that's the problem. She's not thinking logically. When I was told --"

Maddie stopped mid-sentence. Her mind flashed back the two to them on the playground after Mack found out that she was the clone. Mack had asked Maddie what kept her from falling apart. Maddie saw something flicker in Mack's eyes when she responded but hadn't thought about it again until now. The realization made Maddie feel cold. She slumped back down in a chair, trying to shake the feeling that had overcome her.

"Maddie? What's wrong?" John asked, concerned.

"She feels broken," Maddie slowly said.

"Broken?"

"Yes. I didn't see it until now. I didn't see it when she and I were rolling around in the mud on the playground. I didn't see it when she was having her fit in the dorm room. I didn't see it when she was staring off into space. I thought that she felt like she had lost her purpose. Maybe that's it, too, but ... no. Something in the way she acted. I've never seen her like that before."

"Maddie, you aren't speaking clearly," Seth said, watching her closely.

"A lot of people have said how Mack and I are mirror images of each other. So similar, naturally, yet so different. I felt like I had to keep myself together even though there was a part of me that wanted to desperately fall apart. It would have been so easy. Just to stick me with a needle and keep me under medical care until Megan Gatewood was captured. Maybe that is what should have happened."

"Stop." John grabbed Maddie's shoulders as he got down to eye level with her. "You can't take on that burden."

"If I had been under medical watch, Logan would still be alive," Maddie told him.

"You don't know that. The base fell under attack, Maddie. For all we know, if the situation had been different, we all could have died," Seth commented.

"In my head, I know you are right." Maddie slowly turned to meet Seth's green eyes. "I know that. But my heart ..."

"I know. I can still close my eyes and see my brother. But what happened wasn't your fault," Seth told her. "Quit beating yourself up."

"I do know that. I wanted to fall apart then but we were rushed into a battle. There was so many times that I just wanted to crumble but I couldn't let myself. I knew I had to stay strong," Maddie said.

She paused, exhaling deeply.

"I have been told that Mack closed herself off when she became a field agent. She has said before that she felt like she had to for her survival. I have seen a lot of things in the last two years that I never thought possible. Some I wish I could forget. But I never once thought about it changing who I am," she continued.

"Your reactions have been completely different," Seth said.

"Exactly. I opened myself up whereas Mack withdrew into herself. In the park, something inside Mack started to crack. I didn't know it then but I watched her break. She's reaching her shattering point."

"What can we do?" John asked.

"I don't know, babe. Be there for her the best we can, I guess."

# #

The next day, Mack refused to look into Maddie's eyes. The tension between the two women was palpable. Maddie had resigned herself to being the outlet for Mack's anger, hoping that it would help keep her friend together through this mission.

"Is everything okay?" Rachel asked, glancing from Mack to Maddie.

"Everything is fine." Mack gave the tiny woman a weak smile. Maddie nodded in agreement.

"This is important," Rachel pressed.

"Yes, it is," Maddie reassured her.

"Your plight has our undivided attention," Mack stated.

"Good. We are prepared to offer the Fabrega a large supply of neuteroilum in exchange for leaving us alone," Rachel replied.

"Outstanding. That sounds like a great base for negotiations. We'll start with a six month supply and go from there," Mack said.

"I did a little research last night about the neuteroilum. From what I learned, the oil is the base for pluchiot," Maddie chimed in.

"Neuteroilum is needed to synthesize pluchiot, yes, but neuteroilum at its core is only a fuel source," Rachel stated.

"That's what I am worried about. Are you sure that neuteroilum cannot be weaponized?" Maddie asked.

"Our scientists have tried for many years. It's never worked in weapons. It merely serves as a power source for my planet. And the Fabrega are not as sophisticated as we are," Rachel stiffly replied, obviously not liking Maddie questioning her.

"Maybe not the Fabrega, but I figured out a way," Maddie said.

"You did what?" Mack curtly asked, turning toward Maddie.

"In my research last night, I have plans drawn up for the practical usage of a neuteroilum-based weapon," Maddie answered.

"That's impossible. I tried to for years," Mack scoffed.

"And yet, I did it in one night," Maddie murmured shyly, her ears starting to turn pink.

"Give me your tablet. I want to see," Mack ordered.

Mack snatched the data tablet from Maddie's hands before she had a chance to hand it over and began looking over the work Maddie had completed. Her face turned red with anger. Maddie felt like she had just swallowed a stone that sank into her belly. This was not going to do anything to improve Mack's mood.

"She did it. Maddie's right," Mack muttered, her eyes widening in disbelief as she placing the tablet on the table.

"But the Fabrega do not have the same technology at their disposal that you do," Rachel said.

"But there are others that do. I can't in good conscious give an enemy of the ISC something that can be weaponized," Maddie replied.

"You can't do that!"

"I'm sorry, but we can't authorize something which could be potentially dangerous."

"But we have nothing else to offer," Rachel protested.

"Rachel, we will figure something else out," Mack softly promised her.

"Do it soon. The Fabrega will be here before we know it," Rachel said before turning on her heels and storming out as fast as her little legs would carry her.

As soon as Rachel left the ship, Mack started fuming.

"You had no right!" Mack yelled at Maddie.

"No right to do what?" Maddie asked.

"You made me look stupid just now," Mack fired at her.

"That wasn't my intention," Maddie defended.

"Intention or not, you still did. And you took the power away from me in the negotiations."

"Mack, we couldn't give the elements over to the enemy. Both substances have forty times the power that C4 has."

"What are you saying then?"

"I'm saying that it was a bad plan!"

Mack reared her arm back, but Jackson grabbed it before she could throw her punch.

"That's enough out of both of you. Calm down right now," Jackson ordered.

Mack pulled her arm away from Jackson and shot a dirty look toward her counterpart. She let out a low growl from deep in her throat and stormed off. Jackson gave an apologetic glance before following her.

"Talk about if looks could kill," Seth said.

"Shut up," Maddie muttered, exasperated.

"Don't snap at me. I'm just trying to help," Seth replied, throwing up his hands.

"I'm sorry, buddy. I'm just on edge," Maddie apologized.

"I know. We all are." Seth gave her a sympathetic smile.

"We need something to blow off some steam," John said.

"Sounds good. Got any ideas?" Maddie asked.

"Yes, but nothing we can do in public," John answered with a wink.

"Not helping!" Maddie tried to give him a dirty look ended up laughing instead.

"If we were home, we would play paintball," Seth said.

Maddie thought about it for a moment. "We can play soccer or football," she offered.

"Hey now, that's not a bad idea," Seth agreed.

"And the rest of the crews will be here soon to beef up the teams," John added.

"It sounds like a plan to me." Maddie smiled.

#

Several hours later, the teams from Earth arrived and kept their orbit above the planet. Several beamed down to join in on the planned game of football. The groups changed out of their official uniform and met up on the field. Mack elected to not play.

"All right, thanks to everyone who came down to play. This is tackle football. Anyone with a problem with that can beam back to their ship, and no one will think less of you. Well, maybe a little," Maddie joked.

Several of them chuckled at the jab.

"Okay, so let's split up into teams. We don't have any pads, so let's try not to really hurt each other out there, allright? Remember, no punt returns and no extra points. But there are still four downs. Let's have some fun," Maddie encouraged.

Maddie rounded up the guys that they normally played paintball with. Nick, whose nose was still bruised from when Mack broke it, Grant, Will, and Tamma helped to round out their team. The team of eight met up with the second team in the center of the field.

"This is going to be a lot of fun!" Tamma exclaimed excitedly.

Maddie couldn't help but smile. Her enthusiasm was infectious.

They decided that John would be their quarterback. The two teams met to get in formation. The ball was hiked to John as Maddie started running up the field. Seth blocked the tackle attempted on John as the quarterback threw Maddie the football. As soon as she caught it, she was tackled. The referee blew his whistle. Her team achieved first down.

The group got back into their formation on the line where Maddie had gotten tackled. This time John threw the ball to Tamma. Maddie smiled. Tamma was one of the fastest runners she had ever seen in play. With Grant blocking for her, she ran it to the designated end zone.

"Score!" Tamma yelled, spiking the ball and dancing. Maddie couldn't help but laugh.

Since they scored, the ball was turned over to the other team. Grant was not letting the other team get a hold on the field. Nick and Grant worked in tandem, shutting out their opponents. The team went scoreless after four downs.

"Nice job," Maddie told Grant.

"I'm small but I have a low center of gravity. It's hard to stop me once I get going," Grant said with a wink.

"I can see this." Maddie smiled as she nodded.

#

By the time the final whistle blew, the score was 24-12. Maddie's team won. All sixteen players sat down on the grass, taking a moment to catch their breath and relax after the hard fought game. They were all covered with grass stains and dirt from the field.

"Good game, guys and gals," Maddie said, passing out cups of water.

"Just what you needed?" John inquired.

"The steam has been blown." Maddie grinned.

A loud whistle in the distance made nearly everyone jump. Mack emerged from the ship and walked toward them at a furious pace.

"Get cleaned up. Now," Mack ordered with her hands on her hips.

"Calm down, Mother." Nick rolled his eyes.

"I said now, Agent Kicker," Mack sternly said.

"What's up?" Maddie asked.

"The Fabrega are almost here. On your feet," Mack ordered.

CHAPTER SEVEN

After Mack gave the orders, the teams scattered to prepare for the arrival of the Fabrega. One Earth ship landed nearby to assist in case the negotiations got out of hand. So that it wouldn't appear as if they were ready to jump ahead to a fight, Mack ordered all unnecessary ships to the other side of the planet.

"You'd better be in uniform by the time the Fabrega land," Mack snapped, throwing a towel at Maddie's face.

"Hey!" Maddie protested as her counterpart stormed by.

"We don't have time for games," Mack looked over her shoulder. "Get out of these play clothes, put the foolishness of your little football game behind you, and get prepared for work."

Maddie looked over at John, who could only shrug. They quickly showered and got back into their uniforms.

For being a race of small stature, the Agonahans knew how to build … and fast. The large structure that had been a skeleton when they landed was now a completely finished office building. It had been specially designed to handle the three very different races that would be meeting there.

Maddie was amazed by the craftsmanship of the building. The floors were a shiny marble, and the walls and ceiling were made of thick stone. Cedar reinforced the door and two window frames. Everything looked more than twice as large as it should have been, making her feel as small as the Agonahan people. Rachel explained they had to build everything to scale their visitors. The table and chairs were made of a strong, smooth oak. Everything smelled of polished oak and cedar. John climbed into a huge chair and had to help Maddie into hers. They sat with the rest of their team as well as the Agonahan contingents, waiting on the Fabrega to arrive.

Maddie's eyes grew wide as the Fabrega entered. She had been told that they were an ogre-like race, but their appearance still took her by surprise. The Fabrega were a colossal race of approximately eleven feet tall with olive skin, large black eyes, and a protruding jaw. Wisps of black hair stuck out all over the head and the back of the peculiar beings, but no other hair was visible. The room shook as each of the three giant aliens took a step toward the imposing conference table.

"This good," the one who appeared slightly larger than the others spoke in a deep, rumbling voice that reverberated off the walls.

"Teepo, this is Mackenzie and Madison. They are our negotiators," Rachel introduced.

Teepo sized up the two women quickly.

"Yours a puny race, like the tiny ones. Why should Teepo not crush you?" Teepo asked.

"What we lack in physical strength, we make up for in technology," Mack replied calmly.

"Teepo care not for technology. Teepo kill everyone at table," Teepo announced.

"Yes, you could. Yet, you are here. Which means you know that you wouldn't fare well in a gun fight," Maddie said.

Teepo turned his attention to her, letting out a low growl.

"Teepo know this," he agreed.

"Good. So we have an understanding," Mack stated.

"What is it you want, Teepo?" Maddie inquired.

"Teepo wants pluchiot!" he roared.

"No, that's not going to happen," Mack disagreed. "You and I know this."

"Teepo will have pluchiot!" he roared again.

"If puny hum-ans don't give Traylark pluchiot, Traylark will take pluchiot!" another one growled.

"Why do you want the mineral?" Maddie calmly asked, refusing to be intimidated by the large race.

"Need to protect world," Teepo said.

"From whom, Teepo?" Maddie asked.

"From Synth," Teepo replied.

"Teepo, the Synth are extinct," Mack pointed out.

"Synth is alive. Fire on home. Pierce our skins. Kill many, including mate. Vow to return," Teepo explained.

Maddie leaned back in her chair. The Fabrega looked like a fearsome race, but they were merely trying to protect themselves. A part of her felt relieved. This she could negotiate with. Another part of her was concerned about the other race Teepo mentioned. She looked over at Mack whose brow furrowed as the corner of her mouth twitched. She motioned toward Maddie to come closer.

"The Synth are an ancient race thought to have been extinct for hundreds, maybe even thousands of years," Mack whispered in her ear. "Legend has it they had weapons of insurmountable power that could level entire planets to rubble. You remember the planet PS-5478 from a couple of years ago?"

Maddie nodded. It was the planet they ran to when the team rescued Maddie from a shape shifter posing Commander Westlake. The entire planet had been lifeless.

"That was nothing compared to what the Synth were known to do. If they've somehow returned, that could spell bad news."

"Why would the Synth attack the Fabrega?" Maddie whispered back.

"I don't know. Maybe planetary position? The Fabrega's planet is on an edge of the galaxy that borders ours."

"So we've got to help them."

"Yes."

Maddie sat back upright in her chair, collecting her thoughts.

"Teepo, we would like to offer you a place in the Intergalactic Security Commission. If you accept, you will join the federation of planets and will be protected from the Synth," Mack announced.

"Provided that you leave the Agonahans alone," Maddie chimed in.

Teepo stroked his large, protruding jaw.

"Hu-man not protect Fabrega. Synth takes over all worlds," he decided.

"No, Teepo, we are a collection of other worlds joined in protecting the universe. It wouldn't just be us," Mack explained.

"No! Teepo must have pluchiot! Must protect people!" he hollered.

The brand new building trembled as the other two large aliens roared in agreement. The three Agonahans at the table cowered in fear. Maddie swallowed hard, trying to show she wasn't intimated by not breaking eye contact. Mack didn't blink as her jaw set.

"What would you do with the pluchiot if you got it?" Mack folded her arms on the table.

This seemed to stop the Fabregas. They fell silent as they waited on Mack to continue.

"You do not have the means to synthesize the element. What would you do if you were given it?" Maddie repeated the other woman's question.

"Teepo ... Teepo no answer." He hung his head.

"Teepo, we are offering protection. We have the means to synthesize the materials. We can do that for you," Maddie explained.

That made the leader's head snap up in attention.

"You give pluchiot?" Teepo wondered in what could only sound like an eager tone. At least, eager for the Fabrega.

"Will you leave the Agonahans alone?" Maddie questioned.

"You give pluchiot?" Traylark asked.

"Forget about the pluchiot for a second. We are offering you a chance to be in the Intergalactic Security Commission and be under the protection of the collection," Mack said.

"You cheat Siutts! You take pluchiot away!" the third one yelled.

The three Fabrega started to yell again. Rachel's tiny form shuddered as she stared fearfully up at the shouting giants, her head barely peeking over the table. Maddie knew the negotiations were breaking down. She had to do something to avoid a war.

"I have plans for weapons made of neuteroilum which are even more powerful than the pluchiot. I can make weapons that would blow you out of the sky. I will give you the choices that you have. One, you will leave this planet and face the Synth alone. Two, you will join the commission and have allies that will help you against this enemy. Or three, I'll blast your ship to space dust. Your choice."

Maddie folded her arms over her chest as she pressed her lips together and stared indifferent at Teepo.

Everyone at the table fell silent. Maddie's heart pounded in her chest as the options hung in the air. She wiped her sweaty palms on her pant leg, hoping her movements looked casual. She couldn't lose her outward composure now, no matter how much her insides betrayed her. She stared hard into Teepo's eyes, unblinking and unwavering.

"You bluff," Traylark said.

"You can ask these guys, I don't have a poker face," Maddie replied.

"You confuse Traylark," he said.

"I don't bluff," Maddie clarified.

The three frightening beings turned to each other and began to discuss. After several minutes, they turned their attention back to Mack and Maddie.

"Teepo consider offer," the leader announced.

"We eagerly await your answer," Maddie said.

#

"Have you lost your mind?" Mack demanded as soon as the Fabregahad returned to their vessel.

"Sweetheart, no one loves it when you stand up and be a leader more than me, but are you sure this is the right thing to do?" John asked.

"We were losing the negotiations. I had to do something," Maddie responded.

"Madison, are you sure this is a wise course of action?" Rachel asked in her squeaky voice.

"Rachel, I'm sorry, but I really think this will work."

"That's your big plan? To threaten them?" Mack questioned, loud enough to scare the little leader further.

"I called their bluff," Maddie said, standing her ground.

"Just because we have the power to destroy their ship, doesn't mean we want to use it! We are supposed to be doing everything we can to *prevent* the loss of life, not flaunt the ability to end it!" Mack was practically screaming at Maddie.

"Look, they already knew we have the firepower. Teepo admitted to it as soon as they sat down. That gave us the power. They will either join us or back off," Maddie countered.

They climbed down from the tall chairs and started circling each other. Emotions that had been simmering under the surface began to boil.

"You think you are so smart, don't you? You really believe you did the right thing just now?"

"They will back down!" Maddie yelled at her clone.

"What if they don't? Are you willing to put innocent lives at stake over, what, a hunch?"

"You know what? I'm getting real sick of your mouth," Maddie fired back.

"So why don't you shut it, Madison? Or do you not have the balls?" Mack goaded.

Jackson tried to intervene, but John held out his arm. Jackson tried to remove John's hand from his chest but John pushed him back slightly.

"This is between them. They've got to fight it out," John said.

The two women were still circling, sizing each other up.

"What the hell is your problem anyway?" Maddie demanded.

"You! *You* are my problem!" Mack jumped at Maddie, knocking her to the floor.

Mack's hands tightened around Maddie's throat, making it hard for her to breathe. She struggled and clawed before using her elbows to push Mack away from her body and kicked the woman off of her.

"You are your own enemy, Mack, not me," Maddie rasped between coughs.

"You think you are *so* smart," Mack sneered. "You can't see past your own arrogance."

"*I'm* the arrogant one? That's a laugh, coming from you," Maddie scoffed, rubbing her throat.

"What is that supposed to mean?" Mack snapped.

"I'm so great. I'm the measuring stick. You don't compare to me," Maddie mockingly said.

"I *am* the measuring stick!"

"You *were* the measuring stick!"

Maddie couldn't stop herself from screaming at her friend. Maybe this was what Mack needed, someone to yell back at her. Everyone had been treating her with kid gloves since her breakdown at the agency. Maybe what Mack really needed was a good kick in the pants to finally come to terms with everything that's been going on.

"You were the measuring stick," Maddie repeated. "Until I came along and blew you out of the water."

"Please." Mack scoffed at the notion. "You could barely hold a gun before I took you under my wing."

"You may be a better field agent than me, but even you can't deny that I'm smarter than you."

Mack tilted her head back and let out a maniacal laugh."You? Smarter than me? Where do you get off?"

"*I* solved your problem with the satellites. *I* figured out how to recreate neuteroilum weapons when you said it was impossible. *I* did that. Not you," Maddie pointed out.

Mack's dark blue eyes flashed with anger. Her lips curled back in a snarl as Maddie braced herself for an attack. She launched herself at her counterpart, jamming her shoulder into Maddie's stomach. All Maddie could do was hold on to Mack's shoulders as they fell backwards through one of the windows in the conference room.

Glass shattered around them as they landed with a heavy thud. Shards of glass sliced the sleeve of her uniform and blood began to trickle from her left bicep. Maddie could hear the shouts of their teammates as they surrounded them, but no one attempted to separate. Maddie could feel the glass cutting into her back as she rolled Mack off her. She pulled out a huge chuck of glass from her robotic arm and shook bits out of her blonde hair as she stood up.

"You've lost your mind." Maddie shook her head.

"Don't you start on me, Maddie!" Mack shouted, rolling onto her feet. The sound of the grass mingling with the glass crunched underneath the agents' feet.

"Someone needs to. I love you, Mack. I seriously do. But you need to come down off your high horse."

Mack's eyes widened as her nostrils flared with fury. She looked like a caged animal getting ready to strike. Glass shook out of her hair as Mack rolled her neck, feeling the muscles pop in her shoulder.

"I am not your enemy here. I love you. Stop attacking me," Maddie pleaded.

But it was no use. Maddie could tell that her words were falling on deaf ears. The only means she could've reached Mack through had just been closed by their battling bodies. Mack jumped on Maddie, slamming her knees against Maddie's stomach. They fell backward onto the grass. As soon as they landed, Mack pinned Maddie to the ground, using her knees on Maddie's shoulders to ensure she couldn't sit up. She grabbed Maddie's wrists and forced them above her head. Maddie attempted to roll and buck her counterpart off but Mack dug her feet into the ground.

"Get off!" Seth yelled as he knocked Mack away from Maddie.

Mack fell to her side and scrambled to her feet. A low growl erupted in her throat as she punched Seth hard in the jaw. Seth staggered, holding his face as John grabbed his brother by the back of his jacket and pulled him out of harm's way.

"Stay out of this, Seth!" Mack snapped.

"Mack, please," Maddie pleaded, tears rolling down her cheeks. "I don't want to fight you."

"That's too bad. I sure want to fight you." Mack ran toward Maddie.

Before Maddie could defend herself, Mack punched her hard in the face. Maddie gasped as the pain reverberated through her face and more tears swelled up in her eyes. Her hand instinctively touched her cheek, feeling the heat rise on her skin. Mack shoved Maddie away from the crowd, giving them more room.

"Look at you. You are weak. You are pathetic, Maddie. I can't believe we share the same DNA. You embarrass me," Mack bitterly said.

"Say that again," Maddie said in a low, dangerous voice.

"You. Embarrass. Me," Mack repeated.

Maddie finally had enough. She ran toward Mack, using her shoulder to knock her to the ground. She straddled Mack's waist, her punch made contact with Mack's jaw as the other woman tried to toss Maddie off of her. Maddie's stronger, robotic hand grabbed Mack's arm and pinned it to her side. Another punch connected on Mack's face before Mack used her strong legs to flip Maddie onto her back, striking her as well. Maddie threw up her forearms to protect her face. The back of Maddie's hand struck Mack in the face, causing her to whip her head around by the force of the blow then she elbowed Mack in the throat. The mad woman sputtered in shock and pain, grabbing at her throat. Maddie's punch connected with Mack's nose, potentially breaking it, and causing the woman to sputter and roll away from her.

"Had enough?" Maddie asked, breathing heavy.

"You wish," Mack said, getting back on her feet.

Mack grabbed Maddie by her shirt but before she could throw her punch, the sky above them started getting dark.

"What's that?" Maddie asked, looking up.

"You being wrong," Mack bitterly said, shoving Maddie away.

The instant Mack put distance between the, the ground rumbled. Blaster shots rained down, causing explosions around them. Billows of smoke filled the air as chucks of the grass flew up. The wheezing of green fire landed near Maddie. She cried out as the impact threw her into the air, landing several feet from John. Her husband rushed to her side, checking for any injuries.

"Are you okay?" he asked, reaching out to hold her.

"I'm okay." Maddie nodded. "Where's Mack?"

Visibility became increasing more difficult as the once pristine building started to fall apart. Rubbles of marble and insulation crumbled from the conference center. Maddie called out to her clone, but got no response.

"Over here!" she heard Seth's voice call out.

John and Maddie rushed toward his voice, dodging green energy blasts along the way. When they reached Seth, he was kneeling down beside a prone Mack. Dark, sticky blood covered her body. A large gaping wound had split open her side.

Panic washed over Maddie as she tried to cover the hole. Blood washed over her hands when she attempted to apply pressure. She closed her eyes and prayed. *She has to be okay. Please, God. Let Mack be okay.*

"We've got to get out of here. Can you carry her?" Maddie asked.

Seth turned to Maddie. Tears had filled his eyes. "It's no use, Maddie," His voice cracked with emotion.

"No." Maddie swallowed hard. "No, I don't believe you."

Another loud explosion shook the ground hard. Debris flew up over them, but Mack did not move. Maddie knelt on the ground next to her and shook her. John stood above her, acting as a shield while Maddie continued to try to wake Mack.

"Mack." Maddie grabbed her shoulders and jerked her a couple of times, but Mack didn't move. "Mack. Mackenzie."

Mack's head turned toward her. Her eyes were open, but no light shone from them. Maddie slapped Mack's face, but her pupils didn't dilate.

"No," Maddie whispered, not caring about the explosions around them. "No!"

"We've got to get out of here." John pulled on Maddie's arm.

"No! We can't leave her, John!" Maddie cried.

Another blast went off, and the ground disappeared beneath her. Maddie screamed as she slipped away from them.

"Got you!" John exclaimed as he grabbed hold of her hand.

The ground around them had given away. The field where they had played football was no more. The power behind the blasts had broken the land, carving a deep canyon that had cut halfway through the planet. Maddie looked down in shock.

"I can't hold you!" John shouted as Maddie began to slip from his grasp. "Maddie!"

His voice was enough to force her to focus. Maddie used her foot to brace herself against the rock of the planet, giving them leverage. Seth appeared beside John, and together the brothers pulled Maddie back to the surface. John hugged Maddie close to his body. She clung to him, burying her face into his neck. He initialized his communicator cuff, activating the security protocol on their ship to beam them aboard.

#

Safely on their ship, Maddie collapsed immediately on the floor, still shaken from the events. Her entire body felt frozen to the cool metal of the ship as she tried to make sense of it all in her head.

"We've got no time for that." Maddie heard someone say.

"Shields are up. Returning fire," another voice stated.

John sat in front of Maddie, searching her eyes.

"Are you okay?" he asked.

"Okay is relative," she slowly said, her voice barely audible.

"Maddie is in shock," Seth said, his words as far away as her own.

"There's no time," the voice from earlier stressed again.

"Just give her a minute," John said.

"We don't have a minute!" the second voice insisted.

"Where the hell is Jackson?" Seth questioned.

"Maddie, sweetheart, you need to listen to me. We need your help, or we aren't going to make it," John implored her.

"What's...what's going on?" Somehow Maddie managed to get out the question.

"We're on our ship. We're under heavy attack," John explained.

"Mack..." Maddie whispered.

"Jackson just beamed aboard. We've got to move," a voice stated.

"Join up with the fleet," Jackson ordered.

She sighed in relief at the sound of his voice. John scooped up Maddie and strapped her in a flight chair.

"What's the plan?" the second voice asked.

"Those shots are not coming from the Fabrega. Look," John pointed to the view screen.

"The Fabrega ship has sustained heavy damage. There is a large, unknown vessel still firing upon the planet. No damage to that ship."

"David, can you get a reading of the planet?" Jackson asked.

"Yes, sir," David, the first voice Maddie heard, replied. There was a brief pause which seemed to fill the air with tension. "The planet can't take much more of this, sir. The pluchiot is only aiding in its destruction. It's breaking apart."

"All right, how many of our ships are here?"

"Ten are left."

Maddie's head snapped up in alarm. That couldn't be right. There had been twenty-five ships. She found it difficult, but she started to pull herself together. Her mind would have to override the pain in her heart. There would always be time to mourn once they were safe.

"Chris, can you move us closer to the enemy ship?" Jackson asked.

"I don't think that's a good idea. All ten ships are firing on it and not making a dent," the second voice, Chris, answered.

"This ship is outfitted with different shields and weapons," Maddie spoke up, her voice shaking slightly.

Her voice caused the two in the pilot seats to turn around.

"Are you sure?" Chris asked.

Maddie nodded. "I designed it myself."

"Here, allow me," Seth stated, moving over to Chris's chair.

"Be my guest." Chris stood up, gesturing toward the seat.

Jackson and Chris strapped themselves into a flight chair. She ignored Jackson's warning as she unbuckled herself and stood behind the pilot chair.

"You okay?" John asked as he stood behind her, lightly touching her shoulder.

"No, but I need to get us out of this first," Maddie replied.

"What are you thinking?" Seth inquired.

"Move to the starboard side and scan the ship for any weakness," she instructed.

"What do you hope to see?" David asked.

"This ship is outfitted with new sensors, shields, and weapons. It can detect more than others in our fleet. We need to see if we can spot a weakness," Maddie explained.

"You're the boss." David shrugged, not believing her.

After a moment, Seth let out a low whistle. "Scan is complete. I've never seen construction like this. It's pretty impressive."

"It's not matching anything in our data records," David stated.

Maddie leaned over Seth's shoulder, peering at the view screen. She hadn't seen anything like the unknown ship before. It was oblong and gray but it didn't appear to be of any metal configuration she had ever seen before. It almost looked organic to her. The only light emitting from the ship came from the green blaster fire.

"All right, well, that's out. We need to lure the ship away from the planet before--" Maddie began.

A bright flash lit up the entire screen. The shields held but the ship turned to the side. Maddie fell next to the wall, groaning as she hit her head on the metal. She turned as John landed in a thud next to her. The sensors from the control panel lit up and started to buzz. A red warning light flooded the cock pit as Seth and David righted the ship. John and Maddie fell into each other's arms. He quickly checked her over for any bleeding as they stood up. The couple leaned in, resting their foreheads against each other as they struggled for composure.

"Is everyone okay?" Jackson inquired as he unbuckled his safety harness.

John nodded. "I think so."

"Seth, report."

"Uh, Jackson? You've got to see this to believe."

John kept his forehead pressed to hers, rubbing her arms. She kept her eyes closed and held her breath, slowly letting it out.

"I promise once we get home, you and I are going on a vacation," John whispered.

"A real vacation? Are those allowed?" The corner of her mouth twitched. John chuckled, kissing her forehead.

"I love you."

"I love you back."

"Oh, fu … Ma … Maddie?"

The urgency in Jackson's voice made her snap around. He motioned for her to join them. John kept a hand on the small of her back as they walked to the pilot's seats. She gasped, her hand flying to her mouth, as she saw … nothing. Debris was scattered everywhere but the Agonahan planet was gone.

"What the hell happened?" Maddie thought out loud.

"I have no other readings," Seth muttered.

"Damage report?" Jackson asked.

"Minimal damage. Shields are still holding," David responded. "The explosion knocked us way off course. How are we not space dust?"

"The shields Mack and I designed." Maddie's voice cracked slightly. "This is … was Mack's newest ship which she dubbed the *Black Rose*. It's the most advanced in the fleet."

"There are no other ships in our vicinity," Seth stated.

"The force of the explosion must have sent them back as well," John said.

"Or destroyed them," Maddie corrected.

The dark look on Jackson's face was a mixture of disgust and anger.

"I'm sorry, but it's science. The other ships do not have the reconfigured equipment yet, which is why this ship could withstand more than the others. This is still in beta testing," Maddie clarified.

"You mean, this hasn't been fully tested yet?" David asked.

"Well, no." Maddie's cheeks turned pink. "We haven't had a chance to test it in practical applications yet."

The look of anger on David's face made her flush.

"Practical applications, she says. This is our lives here," he snapped.

"Do you have any better ideas?" she asked.

"Not off the dome, no," he admitted.

"Enemy vessel approaching," Seth announced.

John grabbed the back of Maddie's shirt and pulled her gently back into his arms.

"Can we get a second to breathe?" Maddie thought out loud.

"Doesn't look like it. Going into evasive maneuvers," Seth said.

The ship rocked as a blaster shot from the enemy ship hit.

"Shields still holding," Seth announced. "No damage to report."

"Does anyone have a brilliant idea?" John asked.

The ship fell silent. Seth had managed to maneuver the ship to avoid the second blaster charge.

"I think I have it. Fly into that star," Maddie instructed Seth.

"You've got to be kidding me," David said, exasperated.

"The shields will hold," Maddie assured Seth.

Seth looked over his shoulder to Jackson who nodded in agreement with Maddie.

"If Maddie says it will hold, it will."

"Thanks, Jackson." She gave him a small smile.

"I hope you know what you are doing," Seth muttered, setting in the coordinates.

Me, too. Maddie thought. But she couldn't lose her nerve now.

"What's your plan?" Jackson asked.

"We can actually use our shields to deflect energy toward our attackers," Maddie responded.

"That sounds dangerous," John warily said.

"It will take everything we have in shields to do this. We'll only get one shot at this. If my math is wrong, it could destroy us," Maddie admitted.

The crew looked on as Seth punched in the coordinates to the nearest star. The attacking ship began to follow suit. Maddie pulled out her data tablet and connected it to the ship.

"Maddie, please be correct," Seth prayed.

Her entire body shook as she turned on her tablet. Thoughts of Mack kept popping in her head, but she tried her best to push it away.

"Maddie ..." John encouragingly said.

She shook her head. "One minute."

"We don't have a minute, Madison," Jackson sharply said.

"Got it!" she exclaimed, just as the ship entered the star.

The ship began to hum. The shields started pushing back against the star's energy. The enemy stopped its pursuit.

"It's waiting for us to come out," Chris said.

"On my mark, Seth," Maddie said, loading up her newly-written program into the ship's control panel.

"The temperature in the hull is rising," David alerted her.

"I'm aware. We're almost there," Maddie replied.

"I think we have it," Seth said.

"Fire!" Maddie shouted.

Seth pulled the energy surrounding their ship into the weapons system. Thanks to Maddie's new program, he was able to channel the energy toward the enemy ship. The ship exploded upon impact.

"Yes!" David shouted, jumping up from his chair.

John and Maddie happily threw their arms around each other in celebration. Tears of happiness washed her face as she buried her head in his neck. They lingered in each other's embrace until Seth threw his arms around the couple.

"Hull temperature returning to normal. We no longer have use of our shields, but the good news is that the sensors show no other ships in the vicinity," David alerted them.

"You did it!" Jackson exclaimed happily. "Good job, Maddie."

David leaned back in his chair, breathing deeply. "Thank you."

"Set a course for home," Jackson ordered.

"Yes, sir," Seth gladly said, returning to his chair.

Through all the commotion, Maddie hadn't had a chance to really look at their new crew members. Jackson gave the formal introductions. Chris Hicks looked more like a rock-and-roll roadie than an agent. Chris was tall, skinny, and had fair skin. She could see a small tribal tattoo around his right wrist. He had blonde hair which touched his shoulders and clear blue eyes, and stubble covered his chin.

David Haywood was the same height as Chris but with a more muscular build. He looked like he could be a night club bouncer. He had short, dark hair and a full beard. Whereas Chris looked almost pretty for a guy, David was more rugged looking. Maddie smiled gratefully at her new companions.

"Thank you for beaming us off the surface," she said.

"We're glad we caught you in time," Chris replied.

"May I ask how you got on this ship?" she asked.

"We were on the surface when the attack started. I saw that you guys were too far away from your ship to take off, so Chris and I jumped in. We knew we could beam you aboard once we were above the planet," David explained.

"We couldn't run the risk of the ship getting destroyed and all of us getting killed," Chris said.

"It was good thinking. Thank you," John said.

Chris reclaimed his position at the helm as the team regrouped in the small dining area. Now that they were safe, the adrenaline of battle started to wane. The loss of those on the planet was really starting to sink in with all of them. The air was thick with mourning as Jackson sat next to her.

"What the hell happened down there?" Jackson asked.

"I wish I knew," Maddie whispered.

"One second, you two were fighting and the next ..."

"Jackson, I'm so sorry."

He turned his entire body away from her.

"I know … Maddie, I know," he paused, frustration paramount on his face. "It wasn't your fault but I just …can't bear to look at you right now."

"Jackson …" She reached out and touched his elbow but he pulled completely away from her.

"I'm sorry," he said before leaving the room in the direction of the quarters.

Every time Maddie wiped a tear away, two more fell in its place.

Once Jackson cleared the room, John sighed softly. "Is she really gone?"

"I was closest to her when the first strikes hit. She died quickly," Seth mournfully said.

John pulled Maddie into his arms as she started to tremble from her crying. He brushed his fingers through her long hair as her tears soaked to his shirt. No words could comfort any of them. John carried Maddie to their quarters where she cried herself to sleep in his arms.

#

The three day flight back to Earth felt like the longest one of Maddie's life. Jackson wouldn't come out of his room. With him being isolated, it fell to her for command. Regret and sorrow mixed in her heart every time she thought of Mack, which was often. Instead, she used the time to hone her piloting skills with Seth. He had been training her for a few months off and on, getting her prepared for her own ship if Mack's prototype was successful.

She had sent several messages to Commander Levette but hadn't gotten a response yet.

"Isn't that unusual?" Chris asked.

"Very." Maddie nodded. "I hope everything is okay."

"I'm sure we would have heard if something was wrong," John said.

Maddie frowned. Mack's loss weighed heavily on her. The events kept playing over and over in her mind. Mack saw the blast before she did and pushed her out of the way. Mack died to protect her. The realization made Maddie's stomach turn. Just like Logan. How many more people she loved would give their lives? How many more goodbyes did she have in her? Guilt tore at her heart. She had decided to ask for a leave of absence when they returned to the agency. When she told John this, he was very supportive. With everything that had happened, she needed time to deal with the situation.

It felt like things kept piling on top of her. Before she was able to deal with one thing, something else came along. Maddie desperately needed a break. She needed time to mourn.

CHAPTER EIGHT

Jackson was slipping further and further into depression. He wouldn't even look at Maddie. She knew she was pressing her luck, but she had to try to talk to him. She couldn't make peace with Mack. Maybe she could with Jackson. When she went to his quarters to speak to him, she was mildly surprised he let her in but he kept his back to her.

"I'm sorry. It's nothing against you. It's just when I look at you -"

Maddie understood. "I know. You see her."

"She loved you. I hope you know that," Jackson said.

"I do. She was just so angry."

"She was mad over the situation and didn't know how to handle everything so she took it out on the one person she knew would understand and forgive her."

"Yeah ..." Maddie chewed on one of her fingernails. "If I could go back and change anything -"

"Maddie, you can't think that way. None of us can. Believe me, it's easy to dwell. Those kind of thoughts are poison."

"You're right, Jackson." Maddie spit out her broken nail. "Even when she fought me ... I knew. She could have knocked me out if she wanted to."

"Just like you could have knocked her out with your robotic arm. I'm glad that never came into play. We really do need to work on your fighting skills."

Even though his back was to her, Maddie could almost feel Jackson smile.

"Mack saw the blast before I did and shoved me out of the way. She saved my life." Maddie could barely get the words out. "It should've been me who died on the planet."

Tension hung in the air as Maddie quietly sobbed. Jackson's shoulders shook as he hung his head.

"Maddie?" Jackson's voice was so soft she barely heard him.

"Yes?"

"Don't let her regret it."

His words hit her hard. She took a step back, her mind reeling from the pain in his voice.

"I won't," Maddie vowed.

"Can you leave me alone now?"

Maddie wanted to reach out to comfort him but feared it would do more harm than good. She would be there for him if he needed her. She resisted the urge to touch his shoulder as she left him alone in his quarters.

Maddie lay down on the bed in their quarters. John sat down on the edge of the bed. His eyes were red and wet. Maddie wondered how long he had been crying.

"How did the talk with Jackson go?"

"About as good as can be expected, I guess. He let me in but wouldn't look at me."

"I wouldn't take it personally, Maddie."

"It's kind of hard not to, John. I mean, I understand and don't fault him, but it's my face he doesn't want to see."

"Sweetheart, it's not you. It's her."

"I know." Maddie sighed deeply.

"How are you feeling?" He reached over and grabbed her feet, removing her shoes and socks. The boots made a heavy thud sound as it hit the floor.

"Is that a rhetorical question?"

"Don't be like that. We're all hurting here."

"I know. I'm sorry," Maddie sighed again as John began to massage her feet.

"How many questions are swirling around in your brain?"

"Hundreds. None of which I can make any sense of."

"Will talking help?"

Maddie sat up, still keeping her feet in John's lap.

"The Fabrega did not fire on the planet, so who did? The blaster fire was unlike any I have ever seen, John. The planet was cut in half. When the ground gave way underneath me, that hole was deeper than the Grand Canyon. We were lucky we weren't near any pluchiot deposits."

John looked down for a moment as he stopped massaging. "Apparently the others weren't so lucky."

"I can't even think ...we didn't get to say goodbye. We're not going to get to bury her," Maddie sadly said.

"Look at me." John's voice was gentle yet firm.

Maddie looked deep into her husband's eyes as he reached over and tenderly stroked her face.

"You've always told me that everything happens for a reason," he said.

"That is such a cliché right now."

"Does that make it any less true?"

"No, it doesn't."

"What have you taught me, Maddie? We may not always see it, but God is in the details."

"I know." She closed her eyes momentarily. "And I still have my faith. Everything could've been so much worse. Things just don't feel right."

"I know what you mean. It's weird with Mack not being here."

"It's not just that. I have a bad feeling, John. I don't understand it, and I can't shake it."

"My love, you are under a lot of strain right now. We just lost Mack. It's understandable to be out of sorts right now."

But it was more than feeling out of sorts to her. Something didn't sit right.

"I hope that's all it is," Maddie brokenly said.

Seth buzzed through the speaker in the room, asking Maddie to come to the control room. Maddie begrudgingly pulled herself together, trying hard to get into work mode.

#

Seth and David turned around in their pilot's chairs, both of them looking tired, as she entered. Jackson entered silently behind her.

"I thought you'd both would like to see this." Seth motioned her over.

"What's going on?"

"The destruction of the Agonahan planet severely altered our course. I have already compensated for that in our computer."

She nodded. "Good."

"But look." He pointed toward the screen.

Maddie leaned over his shoulder, studying the vastness of space before her."What am I supposed to be looking at?"

"The stars have changed," Seth told her.

"Are you sure?"

"We double checked. What we are seeing here is different than what our systems show," David explained.

Seth pulled up the star charts for her to compare. The difference between the charts and what they were now seeing was undeniable.

"What would cause that?" Jackson asked.

"The system has been affected by the loss of the planet. How much have you had to compensate for?" Maddie asked.

Out of the corner of her eye, she saw Jackson flinch as she spoke. Tension seemed to radiate off of him. He stood behind David's chair, his shoulders and arms tight to his body.

"Quite a bit," Seth replied.

Maddie ignored the discomfort she felt and studied the charts, working the math out in her head.

"More planets have been destroyed. Look," she pointed at the screen. "Three smaller planets are gone. The other planets along here have been altered as well."

"This is interesting. The ripple effect should have been like throwing a rock in the ocean. This is like throwing a boulder in a lake," Chris noted from behind. She jumped slightly, startled by his voice.

"Somehow, I get the feeling that more things have changed," Maddie said.

The ship rocked suddenly, throwing her off guard. Maddie cried out as she fell forward, knocking into Seth. Chris crashed into one of the flight seats behind him. An alert started blaring throughout the ship, indicating that it had taken damage. A red warning light glowed throughout the cockpit.

"Sorry." Maddie's cheeks flushed as she stood up.

"Don't mention it," Seth muttered, rubbing the side of his head which collided with a bulkhead when he caught her.

"Is everyone all right?" John questioned as he entered the room, rushing to Maddie's side. She nodded as she leaned against him, wrapping an arm around his waist.

"Do we have any shields?" Jackson inquired.

"I've been working on it. We only have minimal at best," Seth responded.

"Why hasn't Maddie been working on it?" Jackson questioned. "She is our engineer."

Maddie winced at his harsh tones. Before she could respond, the ship shook again, causing the lights to flicker.

"We were on our way home and weren't expecting an attack. I thought it was best --" John spoke up in his wife's defense.

"Obviously you were wrong," Jackson snapped. "And you are not in authority to give commands."

John's eyes flashed as he squared his shoulders back, getting in Jackson's face.

"Like you've been any kind of authority since we left the planet."

Jackson's nostrils flared as he balled up his fists. Maddie stepped in between them, pushing against John's chest.

"Knock it off, both of you. We're in trouble."

The ship groaned as another shot struck them. An alarm blared throughout the cockpit. Seth yelled out that he lost the engines. The ship shuddered and lurched to the side. Panic filled the room as they were tossed around. The temperature rose significantly as Seth and David tried to right the vessel.

"Seth!" Jackson hollered.

"Working on it."

"Do it faster!"

"Everyone brace for impact."

John hugged Maddie close to him as Seth was forced to crash land on the closest planet to them. She screamed as they fell down, rolling until she hit her head on the console.

"Is everyone okay?" Chris asked.

Maddie sat up from the floor, rubbing her head. "Ow."

"Sorry," Seth apologized.

"It's not your fault." She groaned as John helped her stand up. Relief washed over her as she could see John didn't have any injuries.

"What's our status?" Jackson asked. Blood trickled down from a large gash he had above his eyebrow.

Seth and David reviewed the systems.

"We lost engine one. Hyperdrive is gone. Engine two has sublight capabilities only. We've lost shields," David reported.

"Sensors are badly damaged, too," Seth added.

Maddie's data tablet had been destroyed during the crash. With the systems and their equipment inoperative, the only thing they could do was send out a distress signal.

#

"So what are we supposed to do? Just sit here and wait?" David asked after everyone convened in the debriefing room.

"We don't know exactly what planet we are on. We can only confirm that we are in our solar system," Maddie replied."Tell me, David, how many planets can sustain life in our solar system?"

"Uh ... three?"

"Are you telling me or are you guessing?"

"Um … yes?"

A small smile tugged at the corner of her mouth. "And the nearest to our last known location is home. Which means we are on a planet that is not habitable. This ship will protect us from the elements for a while. Unless you have any other ideas, the best we can do is wait."

"News of the attack and the Agonahan destruction must have gotten back to base by now. So now we just need to wait until a crew comes by and picks up on our signal," Chris said.

"How long can we stay here?" Jackson wondered aloud.

"Without knowing the exact condition of our environment and ship?" Maddie asked.

"Good point," Jackson dejectedly muttered, leaning back in his chai

John propped his feet up on the table. "What I wouldn't give for a cigarette right now."

Maddie's eyes narrowed. "Seriously? That's what you're craving?"

"Don't nag me. I haven't had one in two years and this isn't exactly a walk in the park. Besides," he reached over and grabbed her hand. "All I really need, I have right here with me."

Maddie blushed as he gazed lovingly at her. Passion resonated in his eyes, making her bite her lip.

"All right, you two. Knock it off," Jackson ordered.

She felt embarrassed as Jackson glared at her. *Grief tearing at him as much as guilt was at me.* But when John put his hand on her knee, she closed her eyes briefly, thankful for him, and squeezed his hand.

Feeling restless and not knowing what else to do, John and Seth passed out the food pellet rations they retrieved from the dining hall. Maddie still hated the food pill which represented a meal, but it did the job it was designed to do. To pass the time, the team began to play poker. Maddie listened to the ship creek and groan, deciding it was best to not focus on it and try to enjoy the game.

After Seth dealt the cards, Chris leaned his head to the side. "What is that noise?"

"It's just the ship settling down, man. Relax." Seth organized his cards as he wanted them.

"It sounds like something big is trying to squish us." He looked around the room, running the chips through his fingers.

"There's probably a little extra pressure on the hull. Nothing to worry about." Jackson looked up from his cards and met her eyes for the first time since Mack's death. "Right, Maddie?"

Maddie nodded. "For now. But let's hope our distress signal reaches home before too long."

After two poker games, Maddie grew bored and her mind wandered. Safety protocol has any of the view windows closed so she couldn't see the planet's environment. As the noise from the ship began to increase, she wondered how much more it could take. She prayed the ship would hold out until help could arrive. However, after a few hours, the ship started to rumble and shake.

"That's not good," Chris remarked.

"I don't think it is from the atmosphere," David said.

The ship quaked violently, scattering the cards and poker chips across the table. The alert blared throughout the ship again. The team ran toward the control room as the lights started to spark and dim before going out completely.

"System-wide failure. Activating emergency lights," David said, sliding into a chair.

"Life support is failing. Rerouting life support to this room only," Seth announced as he got in his seat.

"What's happening?" John asked.

"No clue. Sensors are still down."

A violent crash to the side of the ship made it flip over, tossing the crew to the other wall of the ship. The emergency lights flickered before leaving them in pitch darkness.

"So we are completely out of power?" Jackson asked.

"Looks like it," Seth responded.

"Is everyone all right?" Maddie asked.

Sounds of everyone moving around echoed throughout the compartment. Her heart pounded against her chest as she held her breath for a response.

"Bruised but not bleeding," David answered. "At least I don't think I'm bleeding."

"We're sitting ducks," Seth called out.

"John?"

"I'm over here."

In the darkness, Maddie followed John's voice until she found him. He pulled her into his arms tightly and she rested her head on his chest, listening to the rhythm of his heart.

"Everyone, try to slow down your breathing as much as you comfortably can," Maddie suggested.

Now that life support was gone, she estimated they had three hours left before they ran out of air. If they lasted that long.

"Maddie, we could use another one of your brilliant plans," Seth said.

"I'm sorry." Maddie shook her head, even though she knew no one could see her.

The blasts on the hull of the ship intensified. She could feel how fast his heart was pounding against his chest as he kissed her forehead. A finger tilted her chin up and his mouth met hers. She allowed herself to wallow in his embrace, knowing it could very well be their last. No one said a word. Nothing needed to be said.

At least I'll die with John.

Another pair of arms around Maddie from behind. Her head snapped up in surprise.

"Sis, it's me," Seth whispered in her ear.

"Hey, buddy." She wrapped one of her arms around her brother-in-law's waist, holding him to her.

A bright light flashed in the control room, blinding her. Her hand flew over her eyes, trying to protect her. When the light dissipated and her eyes readjusted, they were no longer on their ship. Maddie gasped as Seth peeled away from her, looking around in awe. She still lingered in John's arms. She wasn't sure if she was daydreaming or not.

"What the hell?" Jackson exclaimed.

"This is so cool!" Chris walked around the room. "Is this real?"

"If it's not, then we're all hallucinating," Seth commented.

Maddie observed Jackson looking around the unfamiliar vessel. It was unlike any configuration that she had seen before. Everything looked brand new and clean but she didn't recognize the technology. This wasn't an Earth vessel. Panic rose as she wondered if they went from one danger to another. For all she knew, it could've been the ship firing on them.

"Hello, my friends." The familiar voice was music to her ears.

"Balise?"

"Indeed, Madison," the Isgurd leader replied, stepping further into the room. Alleviation flowed as Earth's first alien friend walked toward her. His wide, black eyes blinked several times before he bowed his bald, gray head.

"Oh, thank God." Maddie's words came out in a rush. She gave John's muscular waist a squeeze.

"Balise, what's going on?" John asked.

"I was able to beam you aboard my ship before yours was destroyed," Balise replied.

She uncoiled herself from her husband's embrace. She brushed her hair away from her face. She looked around the ship, trying to get her bearings.

"Perfect timing!" Seth exclaimed happily.

"Thank you, Balise. Without you, that would have been the end of us," Jackson stated.

"Balise, this is a new configuration," Maddie noted.

"You are correct, Madison. This is a special ship that my kind has never used before," the tiny alien answered. "You are on board its first flight."

"What's the occasion?" David asked.

Balise didn't say anything as his eyes followed the team take in their new surroundings.

"This is some really cool equipment," Maddie noted as she looked at a control panel which lined on the wall.

"Balise, who was shooting at us?" Seth asked.

"Great question. And why haven't we heard from anyone on Earth?" John asked.

Maddie was engrossed in how much more advanced the wall panel was that it took her a few minutes to realize that Balise hadn't answered anyone. She turned and studied him cautiously. He still looked the same as ever to her. His head was much too big on his short, which suited his huge eyes well. Long, skinny arms stuck off from his stocky body. Still, something seemed off. When he finally met her gaze, something in Balise's coal black eyes made her worry.

"What's wrong?" she asked.

Balise blinked but didn't respond.

"Something has happened," Maddie stated rather than asked.

"You are correct, Madison," the little alien finally answered.

Everyone stopped their individual conversations and gave Balise their undivided attention.

"Balise, please," Maddie's voice was bordering on begging.

"What I am about to say is the most difficult news I have ever had the misfortune to deliver," Balise began.

"What's going on?" John implored, stepping over to Maddie and grabbing her hand.

"I have the unfortunate responsibility of informing you that you cannot go back to Earth."

Maddie stared in astonishment. *Can't go back to Earth? What does that mean?* Everyone seemed to begin talking at once, firing questions at him. Balise extended his arms out, trying to bring order.

"What are you talking about?" Jackson questioned.

"The world as you know it is gone. The planet has been overtaken by the Synth."

"That's impossible!" Jackson exclaimed.

"Wait, I don't understand." Chris approached Balise, talking wildly with his hands. "We've been gone, what, two weeks at the most. How could that possibly be true?"

"Yeah, and who is the Synth? I've never heard of them," David inquired.

"I need a minute," Maddie said as she sat down on the floor of the ship.

Jackson stomped over to her, getting down in her face. "Now is not the time."

"On the contrary, Jackson. Now is the perfect time," Balise corrected.

"Back off of her, all right?" John shoved Jackson. "Can't you see she's been through hell?"

"We've all been through hell." Jackson clinched his jaw, but he complied.

Maddie's mind raced. She knew there had been something wrong the moment she saw the Agonahan planet explode. She sat perfectly still on the floor, listening to the ISC's most valued ally explain the situation. John joined her on the floor and held her hand.

"The Synth are a race thought to have been extinct for thousands of years. We do not yet know how they were resurrected, but they have. And the entire galaxy is in danger," Balise stated.

"What exactly happened?" John asked.

"The Synth have developed technology which enabled them to go back in time. They somehow prevented the Intergalactic Security Commission's creation."

The entire team fell silent. Maddie tried to process the new information.

"The agency is gone?" Seth's voice was barely above a whisper.

"Technically, your agency never existed. The only ones of your kind which are safe from them are on this vessel."

"Do you know how this happened?" Jackson asked.

"We believe that the Synth needed the pluchiot from the Agonahan home world to enable them to go back in time. They used beams to extract the mineral, causing the destruction. The attack on the planet was arbitrary."

"That makes no sense," Chris said. "If the agency never existed, then how are we here?"

The realization struck Maddie. "The star."

The team turned to look at Maddie, who still sat on the floor.

"The electromagnetic waves the star created with our shields at the time the planet exploded must have protected us from a shift in the timeline," Maddie answered.

Balise nodded. "You are correct, Madison."

"Then how are you here?" Jackson asked.

"My kind can operate outside of your perceived time and space."

"That's what happened to the other ships," Maddie thought out loud.

"Partially. Some were destroyed when the Synth caused the planet to explode. The others were not protected from the timeline change like you were."

"So, the Synth attacked us?" David asked.

"On the Agonahan homeworld, yes.The latest attack was a planetary droid designed to keep vessels away from Earth," Baliseanswered.

"What's become of our planet?" John asked.

"Most of your kind has been killed in the war. The others have been enslaved, forced to serve the Synth."

"What can we do?" Chris asked.

"I am sorry, Christopher. There is nothing that can be done." Balise shook his head slowly.

Maddie looked bewildered when Balise called Chris by name. She didn't if recall any formal introductions were made.

"So, that's it then? We leave without a fight?" John questioned.

"Jonathan, a fight would result in your death. At least here I can protect you," Balise replied.

"There is another option," Maddie began.

Balise nodded toward her. "I am listening."

"We can go back in time and stop them."

CHAPTER NINE

"Go back and stop them? Are you insane?" David asked.

"Maddie, we don't have the technology for time travel," Chris stated. "Unless you have access to a TARDIS somewhere?"

"You are right, Chris. We don't, but Balise has the ability. Don't you?" she asked.

The crew turned toward the little alien who slowly nodded.

"I do have the ability," he replied.

"Then why haven't you done so already?" David questioned.

"My kind is not equipped for fighting. That would have led to the destruction of my people," Balise responded.

"It's a good thing you have us, then," John said.

"It is indeed." Balise nodded.

"So, this is a real thing? We are really going to do this?" David asked.

"I will need Madison's help to get everything set up, but it can be done."

"Then let's get started," Maddie said, getting up from the floor.

"Are you sure about this?" John asked her.

"What do you mean?"

"This is going to be messing with forces that are beyond you."

"Thanks for your vote of confidence," Maddie bitterly said.

"I'm sorry, but travelling through time delves into physics and space which is beyond your scope."

"Madison is quite qualified, I assure you," Balise said in Maddie's defense.

"You are an engineer," John pointed out to her.

"Engineering is not my only scientific background, John. And besides, since I have been at the agency, I have learned a lot regarding many different fields of research. Balise has faith in me. I would expect my own husband to as well." Maddie pulled away from John angrily.

Maddie followed Balise out of the room.

"Maddie!" John called to her, but she didn't turn around.

#

The doors slid open to a shiny new lab, filled with technology that Maddie had only seen in her dreams. Balise pointed her to a computer console as he climbed into a chair next to her.

"Are you okay, Madison?"

"Hm? Oh. Yeah, I'm fine."

"I would not ask you to do this if I did not think you were capable," Balise said.

"I know." Maddie gave him a gentle smile.

"I am sorry to hear about Mackenzie's death."

"Thank you."

A soft rap on the lab door made her eyes crinkle. She didn't feel like getting into another argument with John, especially when there was so much work to do. She was surprised when the door opened and Jackson stepped in.

"Hey." He looked down at the floor. His hands were in his pockets.

"Hi."

"Balise, could you give me a moment with Madison please?"

"Are you sure?"

Maddie nodded. "It's okay."

The door clicked as Balise closed it behind him. For a moment, tension filled the air as she stared at Jackson. When he finally looked at her, his eyes glistened with fresh tears.

"I wanted to apologize."

"That's not necessary."

"Yes, it is. Maddie, you've done nothing to rise my ire —"

"Except not be her."

Jackson broke eye contact. "Well, that's hardly your fault."

She got up from the table and placed her hands on his shoulders.

"I don't fault you, my friend. Grief can change a lot of perceptions. But the important thing is we still have each other to lean on for support."

His gaze swung back over to her. "You'll help me?"

"Of course. Jackson, we're family. This is what families do."

He hugged her, his body trembling as the emotions poured out. She rubbed his back for a few minutes, whispering words of encouragement. "You loved her with all your heart. And I know how fiercely she loved you. Adoration and devotion like that doesn't disappear after we die. It lives on. You're going to be okay. We all are."

His face was puffy when he let her go. "Thanks."

She gave him a small smile. "Anytime."

He left a few moments later. Balise studied her as he reclaimed his position by the transporter console. Maddie stared blankly at the computer screen, not sure how to begin.

"Are you sure you are ready to proceed?" Balise asked.

"Yes," Maddie replied, putting more confidence in her voice.

"Good. Because this is going to be difficult."

"Nothing important is ever easy," Maddie agreed.

"We are going to modify the transporter protocols."

"Okay." Maddie chewed on her bottom lip as she pulled up the schematics. Balise started to disassemble the transporter while Maddie studied the plans. "This is going to be a one way trip."

He nodded. "Yes."

"So we'd better be right."

"Yes."

"Do we know when?"

"The Intergalactic Security Commission was established in 1965 after an experiment caused Charles Westlake to interact with my kind for the first time."

Maddie was surprised. "Charlie? Wow."

"Indeed. Charles was thirteen years of age at the time but had a mind beyond his years. We had ignored your planet, thinking that your kind was too primitive. Charles created a communication device which allowed him to make contact with a passing ship. We landed and opened communications with your government. The rest, as they say, is history," Balise explained.

"I never knew that Charlie had such a big role in the creation of the agency."

"Without your former commander, the Intergalactic Security Commission would not exist."

"So that's what happened. The Synth went back in time to stop Charlie from creating his device."

"The Synth killed him before he could make his device work."

"So we need to go back and prevent the Synth from killing Charlie."

"That is correct."

Something came to mind as she studied the functionality of the transporter. If they were able to stop the Synth, then Mack would be alive when the timeline was restored. That thought strengthened her determination to make everything right.

Her brow wrinkled as she learned all that she could about the schematics. The transporter was much different than the ones that were currently used on the ISC's ships. The transporters worked by controlling matter and energy, breaking down both at the molecular level and reassembling it based on the destination coordinates. One mathematical mistake would kill someone.

Maddie remembered Mack explaining it to her two years ago. Mack had been the engineer who worked with Balise on configuring the system for human DNA, so they could have the technology on their ships. Her work had been limited only to give the transporter system to the human ships.

The difference between the transporters configured to work on human ships and Balise's was that his also operated with a time variable. Since his species operated outside of the normal definition of time and space, the time variable was necessary for his transporter to work. With this in mind, Maddie set to work on the mathematical equation to get his transporter to support their human DNA.

#

"Maddie," John's raspy voice gently called to her. "Babe, wake up."

Maddie slowly lifted her head from the lab table. *How long have I been asleep?*

"Huh?" Maddie groggily asked.

"You passed out, sweetheart."

Maddie wiped some drool from her cheek as she stretched her stiff neck. John pushed the laptop away from her and massaged her shoulders.

"What time is it?" she asked.

"Three in the morning," John told her.

Balise had fallen asleep on the floor, surrounded by computer components. Maddie stifled a giggle.

"Come to bed. It'll be easier to think in the morning," John encouraged.

Maddie tried to stand, but her knees buckled. After sitting on the wooden stool for hours, her legs refused to work. John caught her in his arms and carried her out of the lab.

"I'm going to save her," Maddie said into his muscular chest as they walked to their room.

"Who?" John asked.

"Mack. I'm going to fix it," Maddie groggily told him.

"How?"

But Maddie was drifting back asleep. He used his thumbprint to open their quarters and voice activated the lights. John gently laid her on their bed and curled up next to her. For the first time in weeks, they both got a peaceful night's rest.

As the team gathered together for their breakfast, Maddie informed them about the plan. A member of Balise's crew named Vanda joined them. From what Maddie had observed from walking around the ship, each member of his race looked exactly alike. She couldn't tell any of them apart, nor could she tell the sex of any of them. Vanda's voice wasn't as deep as Balise's, making Maddie wonder if Vanda was a female.

"According to Balise, the Synth went back in time to stop the formation of the agency. We are working on the transporters to get us back there," Maddie explained.

"I'm sorry, I know I'm a soldier, not a scientist, but how do you plan on getting us back in time and stop this incredibly advanced ancient race?" David asked.

"I've figured out how we are going back. We need to protect Charlie Westlake once we arrive. He's the key to this whole thing," Maddie responded.

"And how do you plan on protecting him?" Chris wondered.

"We've seen the destruction of the Agonahan home world. Their weapons are far superior to ours," Jackson pointed out.

"I understand that, but the only way to restore the timeline is to protect Charlie. He's the one that makes contact with Balise's race and gets the ball rolling on the formation of the agency," Maddie said.

"All right." Seth nodded. "Now we understand what we have to do, how do we do it?"

Maddie chewed on her bottom lip. Hundreds of different scenarios played out in her mind. Somehow, they needed to be prepared. The future of their planet and countless others depended on them.

"We know the year the Synth went back in time, but we don't know the date. Maybe some research will help in that matter," Maddie said, thoughtfully.

"Right. There must be a record somewhere when the Synth took over Earth," Jackson agreed.

Chris's hand shot up in the air. "I can do that."

Maddie raised an eyebrow as Chris eagerly looked at her.

"I thought you were a pilot," John said.

"I am but before then, I was Charlie's researcher. I owe him, Maddie. Let me do this," Chris pleaded.

She was choked up as his emotions poured out. *We all owe Charlie.* "All right. Head off to the lab and see what you can find out."

Chris beamed as he ran his fingers through his blonde hair. He jumped out of his chair and headed for the door.

"Chris?"

He stopped and turned around at the threshold. "Yeah, Maddie?"

"Make him proud."

"You bet."

"All right, how do we stop an advanced race with superior weapons hell-bent on controlling the galaxy?" David asked.

"Maybe Balise can give us weapons and -" Seth began.

Maddie shook her head. "Out of the question."

"Why?" Seth demanded.

"We are looking to restore our timeline. Any number of things could happen. Are you familiar with the butterfly effect? We could end up changing things in our timeline we didn't mean to. And we can't keep going back in time to fix it. Absolutely not," Maddie stated.

"Come on!" Seth slapped the table. "We should fight fire with fire."

"Buddy, I love your enthusiasm but that's not the way to go."

"We need to keep a low profile once Maddie and Balise manage to get us back in time. If this battle goes public, the last thing we need is weapons from a different time. If our government were to confiscate the weapons --" Jackson countered.

"I get you," David cut in, ruffling up his dark hair. "Butterfly effect."

"Exactly. Whatever we do, we need to do so discreetly. We won't be doing anyone any favors if we get captured."

"Maddie, you said you figured out a way to make a weapon out of the neuteroilum," John stated.

She nodded. "I did."

"Would it be possible to somehow make a gun with the neuteroilum that would look like a weapon from that era?" he asked.

She pressed her lips into a thin line as she pondered."It's possible, I guess. I couldn't say for certain without some neuteroilum, and the only resource is gone."

"We do have a little bit of neuteroilum on this ship," offered Vanda.

"A little is all I need," Maddie said.

"Very well." Vanda nodded.

"Will it work?" Jackson asked.

"I'm pretty sure," Maddie replied.

"Maddie, I don't need pretty sure. I need you to be positive," Jackson sternly said.

"I'm positive that I'm pretty sure it will work," Maddie replied.

Jackson gave her a dirty look. She answered his glare by sticking out her tongue.

"I can't speak in absolute terms until I test my theory, Jackson."

Jackson grinned. "Ever the scientist."

"It's what I'm built for," Maddie agreed.

"So, in theory, what is your plan?" David asked.

"I should be able to lace the bullets with the neuteroilum which will give us the handheld power of a bazooka," Maddie stated.

"Won't that be dangerous?" John questioned.

"Highly. And destructive, I might add. But I do feel like it's our best chance against the Synth."

"Then let's get to work," Jackson encouraged, as he adjourned the meeting.

CHAPTER TEN

Maddie wished Mack or her assistant, Hunter, was with them. Hunter knew how to anticipate Maddie's needs so she didn't have to ask for much in the lab. She was thankful for Chris and David, who had become willing assistants. Plus, it gave her a chance to get to know them as she built a pair of robot arms.

David had been a bouncer in a country bar in North Carolina when he had been asked to join the agency. He spoke of Charlie fondly, talking about how the former commander had seen something more in him than just a bouncer. He occasionally ran a hand over his hair as he talked about his home. Chris had been a low level researcher for a cell phone manufacturer when Charlie asked him to join.

"Charlie recruited you?" she inquired.

Chris nodded. "Don't know how he found me, but I've always been glad he did."

The thought occurred to Maddie how different the stories were from everyone she talked to about how they joined the ISC. No one came from a military background. Charlie had done a lot of recruiting and he seemed to find something special in just about everyone. This made Maddie more determined than ever to save his life.

"This is going to work, Chris. We're going to save Charlie."

"I'll finally be able to return the favor." Chris flashed a grin as he handed her a tool Maddie had pointed to. "How is it coming?"

"It's been a while since I've worked with robotics. I didn't realized how much I missed it until now," she said.

To create the neuteroilum weapon, the robot arms were critical to her experiment. The neuteroilum was too volatile in its form to be touched by human hands. She programmed the robotic hands to brush the oil on the bullet with the gentlest of touches. The robot would work inside a container that, in theory, would protect them should the oil become explosive.

"Vanda, how goes that shatterproof glass?" Maddie called out.

"I must correct you, Madison. No glass is shatterproof," Vanda advised.

"Forgive me." Maddie took a breath, to make sure she didn't sound sarcastic. "How is the crystalline substance which should help contain an explosion coming along?"

"Very well," Vanda answered.

Maddie looked up from her robotic arms as she watched Vanda. The little alien continued to stare at her, as if not sure what Maddie was waiting for.

"When can I have it?" Maddie asked.

"Shortly," Vanda replied.

Maddie tucked some of her long hair behind her ear, taking a deep breath. Vanda was getting on her nerves, but Maddie knew being snarky or snapping was not going to help the situation. It would only irritate her further and be lost on Vanda.

She had intended to control the robotic hands herself, but Jackson and John argued with her.

"I can do this," Maddie insisted. "I do know how to work robotic limbs."

"I know you do, sweetheart, but —"

"Hello!" Maddie rolled up her sleeve on her right arm and exposed the synthetic skin. She pulled at it just enough to expose the wiring. "I'm part cyborg."

The skin snapped back into place and Maddie put her hands on her hips. John ran his tongue across the bottom of his lip, chuckling. Jackson elbowed him in the ribs and he cleared his throat.

"It's too risky, Maddie. I don't want you to do anything that might endanger your life," John pleaded.

"You think *I* would do anything which could hurt me?"

"John's right. It is too risky. I'm not going to allow it," Jackson agreed.

"Since when did you become boss?" Maddie demanded.

"When Mack was killed." Jackson's tone was deep and rough. She knew better than to challenge him.

"Fine. But I'm not happy with this," Maddie conceded, pointing her finger into Jackson's chest.

"Noted."

She felt like grumbling but didn't see how that would make a difference. Deep down, she knew they were both right. She created a computer program that would control the robotic arms via a platform console to appease both men.

#

Once Maddie had finished the work on the robotic, and Vanda completed the protective case, she began the delicate task of coating the bullets.

"That gun doesn't look any different than ours." David pointed to the guns lined up on Maddie's work table.

"Thankfully, gun design hasn't changed all that much in the last fifty years," Maddie replied.

As Maddie made her first attempt to brush the oil onto the bullet, the right robot arm dropped too soon after brushing and knocked into the tip, causing an explosion. Maddie let out a loud gasp. David covered his ears. Maddie let out a sigh of relief that the protective casing held.

"Can we try that again?" David loudly questioned with his hands still over his ears. "Only this time without the boom?"

"This wouldn't be so difficult if I could manually control the robot," Maddie grumbled.

He winced as he looked at her then nodded at the casing. Maddie rolled her eyes and pulled his hands away from his ears.

"It's okay, David."

David ruffled his shorthair, the way Maddie noticed he tended to do when he was nervous. "You and John, you happy?"

"Immensely," Maddie responded.

David stroked his thick black beard and nodded.

"Do you have someone?" Maddie inquired.

"Her name was Maria. You are lucky that yours is here with you."

"I know. I don't take it for granted."

"Don't. Don't do it. Not even for one second."

"Where was she?"

"She was on one of the ships. She was a pilot, too."

Maddie patted David's forearm soothingly, but he gently shrugged her off.

"This plan of yours better work," he said.

"You know I wish I could promise you that it would."

"I do. Let's ... let's just do what we do best."

"Put an explosive element on a weapon?"

"Kick some enemy alien butt," David said with a grin.

It took them several more tries without incident, but Maddie and David were able to put the neuteroilum onto the bullets successfully.

"Where are you going?" David asked as Maddie took off her lab jacket and protective goggles.

"To bed."

"Shouldn't you be working with Balise on the transporters?"

"David, I'm exhausted. I need a break."

"But the transporters --"

"Will still be there after a few hours of sleep. We've got nothing but time right now."

A low sound deep in David's throat let her know he wanted to argue with her. She shook out her blonde mane and sighed. "David, once we activate the transporters and go back to 1965, we don't know what's going to happen. I need a little time with my husband before then."

David stared hard for several moments before he leaned against the lab table. He seemed to visibly relax. "See you in the morning."

"Get some rest. You are no good to me asleep on your feet."

"I thought Jackson was the squad leader?" A teasing smile tugged at the corner of his mouth.

"Details." She grinned.

#

As soon as she walked into their quarters, Maddie belly-flopped on the bed.

"Tired?" John asked, looking amused.

Instead of replying, Maddie groaned into the pillow. John chuckled, and then straddled her back.

"What are you doing?" Maddie asked as John rolled up the back of her shirt to her shoulders.

"Massaging you," he replied as he unhooked her bra.

"Babe, that's really not nece -" Moans drowned out the rest of her sentence.

"Yeah, that's what I thought." John chuckled. "You're entire body is tense, love."

"Wonder why."

Maddie rose up on her elbows long enough to take off her shirt before lying back down.

"Just relax. I'm going to take care of you." John's voice was as smooth as silk.

He trailed kisses from the base of her neck down her spine to her lower back. Maddie's skin heated under his touch. His hand slipped under her, caressing her flat stomach, then dipped down to her hip. In one swift motion, he turned her over. She bit her lip as she looked up at him. His eyes darkened with desire as he bent down to kiss her. The trouble they were in, the upcoming dangers -- everything disappeared in that instant. His scent filled her nostrils as he kissed under her left ear. Their bodies molded together in the familiar rhythm as their passions increased.

Maddie curled up on John's arm after their passionate lovemaking. She twirled a few strains of his copper hair as she watched him lie peacefully beside her.

"Are you enjoying that?" He didn't open his eyes as he grinned.

"There isn't a thing about you that I don't enjoy."

"Insatiable woman."

"Only for you, love."

John slowly opened his eyes as he turned toward her, stroking her cheek. His finger traced the scar left behind when her face was slashed with a whip years ago.

"I really would be lost without you," he whispered.

"You'll never have to worry about that," she said, running her hand up and down his arm.

"We're going to make it through this."

"I wanted to talk to you about an idea I had."

John's face changed instantly to a serious expression.

"You have my attention," he said.

"I've been thinking. There is a reason why even the Isgurd don't travel in time. It's dangerous."

"What are you thinking?"

"Would it ... would it be so bad if Mack thought I was still her clone?"

"Maddie ..."

"No, hear me out. She was shattered, John. The news broke her. I had never seen her act like that."

"You have a beautiful heart, and it's in the right place. But, Maddie, you don't know what could happen."

"I know ..."

"We can't do anything except prevent the Synth from killing Charlie."

"I know. You're right, John."

"But?"

"No buts."

John studied her face for a minute, clearly not convinced.

"But what if Mack isn't able to come back from this?" she finally continued.

"She will. But we have to give her a chance."

"You are right," she reluctantly agreed.

"I know. And if you asked Jackson, he would tell you the same thing."

Maddie wrinkled up her nose, hating to admit that he was right. In response, John kissed the tip of her nose.

"Do you feel like sleep, or are you up for round two?" John asked.

Maddie pretended to consider the options for a moment. "Round two."

John and Maddie joined the rest of the team the following morning. Everyone was dressed in simple slacks and plain t-shirts to blend in with the timeframe. Maddie pulled her blonde hair back in a simple braid while all the men slicked their hair back.

"I don't like this." Maddie tugged on John's hair.

He shrugged. "It was the style back then."

"Are we ready for this?" Seth asked.

Maddie looked down at Balise, who nodded in approval.

"The transporter is ready whenever you are. I must warn you to be careful. We will not have a second chance to attempt this. Once you are successful, I recommend you find a quiet place to settle and do not do anything that will affect your timeline," Balise warned.

Jackson started passing out the guns. "We each have a few magazines that we can store on our bodies, but only the magazine inside the gun has been painted with the neuteroilum. Please use extreme caution."

Everyone grabbed a holster and attached it to their belt. The team then stuffed extra magazines in an attached pouch on their belt. Maddie rolled up her pant leg and strapped a knife to her ankle. She looked around the room as everyone prepared and watched several others also conceal knives.

Maddie had been so focused on the prep of the mission, she hadn't thought much about the mission itself. They were getting ready to travel back in time to stop an ancient, alien race. She didn't even know what the Synth looked like. The weight of the mission struck her. She swayed as her head began to spin. The ground gave under her feet, and she couldn't stop herself from falling. John caught her before she hit the ground.

"Maddie!" John called out in concern. He gingerly sat her down in a chair. "Seth, can you get Maddie some water?"

"I'm on it."

"I'm fine," she said weakly.

"No, you're not. You are sweating." John patted her forehead with a towel.

Maddie's heart was racing. Color drained from her face. She couldn't focus on anything.

"Lean over, place your head between your knees, and breathe," Jackson instructed.

"I ... I can't." Maddie's breathing was raspy.

"Yes, you can." John placed a gentle hand on the back of her neck and guided her down.

Maddie struggled for a few minutes to breathe before she was able to get back to normal. She gradually felt like she was regaining control. Slowly, she sat up again.

"Are you okay?" John asked, studying her carefully.

"I think so."

She gulped down the water Seth handed to her as she steadied herself. John tilted her chin back, forcing her to meet his gaze.

"Don't lose your nerve on me now. We're going to get through this, but only if we all stick together."

"Okay ... okay ..." Maddie nodded, breathing deeply.

"We can't have you flipping out on us now," David said.

"I'm sorry, guys. I'm all right," Maddie assured them.

"Madison, there is an important detail that you must know before you leave," Balise said.

"And what's that?" she asked.

"Our records show that Charles Westlake died in 1965, but the Synth did not reveal themselves until 1970," he told her.

"Five years? Why did it take them five years?" Maddie wondered.

"We do not know," Balise said.

"Well, that's something less to worry about," Jackson said.

"I'm not following." Seth shook his head.

"It means we have a window of opportunity." Maddie nodded in agreement with Jackson.

Seth stared blankly at them. "I'm still not following."

Maddie studied their little alien friend carefully. Five years. The Synth's mission to stop Charlie from contacting the Isgurd was successful, but it still took them five years to reveal themselves and take over Earth. A plan started to formulate in her mind. Balise slowly nodded toward her, almost as if he could read her thoughts. *I wonder if he can.* Balise nodded again. *Hmm... maybe he can.*

"I guess we'll figure it out when we get there," she said.

The team gathered tightly in a circle. The shaking in Maddie's hands were only calmed when John gripped hers. Jackson gave the order to begin transport. Warmth enveloped over the group before they were surrounded by a bright white light. Maddie's stomach lurched as the familiar feeling of the teleportation overcame her. All of her senses were lost to her as the ship faded away.

CHAPTER ELEVEN

The entire team let out a sigh of relief when the transport was successful. Maddie blinked several times as their new environment became into focus. The humming sound of the ship changed to birds chirping in a nearby tree. Maddie closed her eyes as she felt a cool breeze pass by. It felt like it had been eternity since she stepped foot on soil.

"Where are we?" Chris asked.

"Charleston," Maddie responded.

The team looked around, trying to get a landmark for their surroundings.

"How can you tell?" David asked.

"That's the park where my clone likes to take Lucas." Maddie pointed to the left.

"What now?" David's eyes grew wide at her admission.

Maddie's ears turned pink. "My son … it's a long story."

The houses surrounding the park looked eerily familiar to her. Everything was pretty much the same as she remembered, except newer. She scanned the area, watching for anything out of the ordinary. No one seemed to notice the six of them seemed to appear out of thin air.

David asked the question that was on everyone's minds. "Okay, we're here. Now what?"

"Yeah, how exactly do we find Charlie?" Chris asked.

"Well, how many Westlakes could be in the phone book?" John wondered aloud.

"Brilliant. So we locate his address, and then what? We go knocking on his door?" Jackson scoffed at the notion.

"Then what precisely would you have us do, genius?" John challenged.

"Here we go again." Seth sighed.

Maddie was barely listening to the men bicker. There had to be a reason why the transporter dumped them out on this spot. Her eyes searched the area, spotting a group of teenagers near the baseball field which sat at the edge of the playground.

"Hey, guys." Maddie snapped her fingers to get their attention.

John and Jackson stopped arguing and turned to her. "What?"

Without saying a word, Maddie started walking toward the direction of the teenagers. The group looked like they were beating on something. She could hear cries from someone in the pack. Maddie broke into a run, pulling one of them away from the pack.

"Hey, back off!" the teenager exclaimed.

"That's enough," Maddie snapped.

Upon seeing her, the pack stopped their assault. By the time John reached her, the group had completely backed off.

"It's all right, man. We're cool," one of them said.

Maddie kept her eyes on the retreating pack until they were a safe distance away. She looked down to see a small, frightened boy who looked around thirteen. He had sandy blonde hair, big round brown eyes, and freckles dotting the bridge of his nose. His wire-framed glasses had been bent. The boy's nose and lip had been busted, his baseball jersey torn.

"Are you okay?" she gently asked.

The boy nodded. "Thank you."

Maddie extended her hand and helped him up.

"Are you an angel?" the boy asked.

Maddie couldn't help but grin at him. She dusted off his back and straightened his glasses.

"No, sweetie. My name is Maddie Brooks. This is my husband, John," she introduced.

"Charlie Westlake," he confirmed.

CHAPTER TWELVE

Before departing with Charlie, Maddie and John talked it over with Jackson. The others would keep a safe distance, to make sure not to overwhelm him. Maddie and John would be his point of contacts.

"The less we interact with him, the better we can ensure less mistakes," Jackson said.

Maddie nodded. "I agree."

"Use your wrist comm open if there is trouble. We'll meet up later."

Maddie nodded, touching the metal band on her wrist. Jackson slapped John on his shoulder and grinned. The couple walked over to Charlie who was watching the others with scrutiny.

"Who is that?" He nodded to them.

"Just a few friends of ours," Maddie replied.

They started walking to Charlie's house which was several blocks from the playground.

"Are you sure you're okay?" Maddie asked.

Charlie nodded. "Thanks to you. Are you sure you're not an angel?"

Maddie's cheeks began to turn pink. "No, but thank you."

"You sure look like one."

John nearly laughed at the way Charlie was looking at Maddie full of admiration. He seemed like he was quickly developing a crush.

"Why were those teenagers attacking you?" John asked.

Charlie looked John up and down, regarding him coolly.

"We lost the game because of me. They jumped me afterward," Charlie explained.

Maddie looked at him sympathetically. Charlie smiled at her then shrugged.

"I tried to tell my dad that sports aren't my thing, but he insisted I sign up. The boys my age are all bigger than me anyway. It's not fair," he complained.

"What is your thing, Charlie?" Maddie asked.

"Science." He grinned. "I love it. I'm going to be a scientist one day."

"Oh, yeah?"

"I'm actually working on an experiment," Charlie admitted.

"What kind of experiment?" John inquired.

Charlie glanced over at John, distain still in his eyes. "If you must know, I'm working on a communications device."

"What kind?" Maddie asked.

"Something strong enough to reach outer space. I'm hoping to bounce a signal back from the moon," Charlie enthusiastically said.

"If you set your mind to it, you will," she said.

Charlie's eyes widened. "You really think I could be a scientist?"

"Absolutely. I think you can," she encouraged.

"Glad you think so." Charlie frowned. "My dad seems to think science is silly. He says it's a waste of time."

"Nothing you love doing is a waste of time, Charlie." John lightly touched his shoulder. "Don't let anyone make you feel guilty for it."

The distrust Charlie had in his eyes drifted away. "Thank you."

"I think if you work hard, you can do anything. That's what I did, and I'm a scientist."

"But..." Charlie looked at her skeptically. "You're a girl."

Maddie laughed. "Girls can be scientists, too."

"Name one," Charlie challenged.

"Dorothy Hodgkin," Maddie automatically told him. "She won the Nobel Prize last year in chemistry. This year, she won the Order of Merit."

John looked over at his wife in surprise but didn't say anything. Her mouth twisted into a smirk, winking at him.

"What about in physics?" Charlie questioned.

"You mean, other than me?" Maddie asked.

Charlie's jaw dropped open. "You're in physics?"

Maddie nodded. "My sister and I both are."

As soon as she said it, Mack's face appeared in her mind. She quickly pushed it away, trying to stay focused on Charlie.

"That's so cool!" Charlie enthusiastically exclaimed.

Mentioning Mack seemed to be enough to pacify Maddie's claim of being a scientist to him. Charlie started firing away questions to which Maddie happily answered without giving away too much information.

They walked up to Charlie's home, meeting his mother on the front porch.

"Charlie!" she woefully cried at the sight of his disheveled appearance. "What happened to you?"

Brushing back the length of her dark blonde hair from her face, Charlie's mother tugged on his torn clothes. She took a knee in front of Charlie, gripping his arms anxiously.

"Cool it, Mom." Charlie pulled away when she tried to touch his face.

"He was jumped in the park," John said.

The sound of John's voice made her jump and turn around. Her eyes filled with shock as she looked over the couple.

"What's going on? Who are you?"

"Mom, they helped me. This is Maddie and John Brooks," Charlie introduced.

"You ... you saved my boy?" she warily asked.

John nodded. "We thought it best if we walked him home, just to be on the safe side."

His mother placed her hand over her heart and relaxed at John's words. She rubbed her hands on her apron before offering them a handshake.

"My name is Sandy. Thank you for looking out for my son."

"Mom, can they stay for dinner?" Charlie asked.

"Oh, no. We wouldn't want to intrude," Maddie said.

"Nonsense!" Sandy waved her off. "Please, won't you join us?"

John and Maddie exchanged a glance before agreeing.

"Great! I'll go set two more places at the dinner table. Charlie, go clean up."

Maddie was a little nervous as they headed into the house. A long couch with yellow floral print took up most of the small, yet comfortable living room. Charlie's father sat in a matching recliner, his eyes narrowing as they entered.

"If you're selling something, we're not buying," he roughly told the couple.

"Oh, no, sir." Maddie gave him a warm smile. "My name is Maddie Brooks, and this is my husband, John."

"Humph," he grumbled, taking a sip from his canned beer. "You look like a stinking door-to-door salesman.

"Murphy, be nice." Sandy admonished, returning to the room. "These are our guests."

"Guests? What for?" Murphy muttered.

"Sweetheart, they saved Charlie from a beating in the park," Sandy answered.

"Bah!" Murphy rolled his eyes, waving his hand to dismiss her comment. "They should've let him get roughed up. It'll teach him something."

"Murphy!" Sandy looked shocked at her husband. "That's our son you're talking about."

"I'm well aware, Sandy. But you baby him. The boy needs to toughen up if he's going to make it in this world."

Sandy muttered something under her breath before turning her attention back to the uncomfortable couple.

"Maddie, John, you are welcome here. Dinner is ready."

Murphy griped as he rose from the recliner, giving the couple a dirty stare as he passed. Sandy sighed, giving them an apologetic glance.

"Things have been tough since Murphy got laid off down at the plant. Please don't mind him," she whispered.

Maddie looked to John, giving him a nervous smile as she reached for his hand. This was going to be a very awkward dinner, but a necessary one to gain Charlie's trust.

#

"So," Murphy's rough voice rumbled as he scooped spaghetti into a bowl. "If you aren't salesmen, what do you do for a living?"

"Well," Maddie looked over at John and chewed on the inside of her cheek. "I'm a scientist."

"A scientist?" Murphy dropped his fork, looking at Maddie in surprise. "You? No offense, darling. You're too pretty to be a scientist."

"Um, thank you." Maddie supposed she should take that as a compliment. Her hands shook slightly under Murphy's stare, but she took a deep breath and gave him a polite smile. "Actually, to be more specific, I'm a physicist and an engineer."

"What's the matter, honey? Wasn't being taken seriously in one field, so you pursued the other?"

"Murphy!" Sandy exclaimed, her cheeks flushed. "I'm sorry, Maddie. He doesn't mean it."

"Like hell, I don't. There's not enough jobs to go around, and this woman is taking two." Murphy groused. Ice swirled around in his glass as he stirred sugar in his tea. "I suppose you want me to call you Doctor."

"Actually, no. I don't have my doctorate," she said.

"Weren't smart enough, eh?"

Maddie felt fire in her cheeks at his words, opting to shovel spaghetti into her mouth instead of responding. John, however, balled his hands up into fists, his knuckles turning white. He pushed the plate away from him.

"She decided to focus her time on other things," John hotly said. Maddie covered her hand with his, giving him a pleading look.

"Other things? Like what?" Murphy pressed.

"Perfecting the quantifying qualitative data methods," Maddie shyly replied.

Murphy shook his head. "Sweetheart, I have no idea what you just said."

"Dad, you're embarrassing me." Charlie gritted his teeth.

Murphy cut his eyes to Charlie. The teenager mumbled a word of apology and looked down at his food.

"I should've gotten my doctorate. I often wished I had," she admitted, pulling Murphy's attention back to her.

"Don't get down on yourself," John said, giving her hand a squeeze before turning his attention back to Charlie's father. "Maddie is a brilliant scientist."

"I'm sure she is. And if brilliance paid the bills, we would all be millionaires." Murphy picked up his glass of tea and brought it to his lips.

"Some of us more than others," John snapped back.

Murphy paused before he took a drink. "You talking down to me at my own kitchen table?"

"Hey, everyone please calm down," Sandy said, standing up at the table.

Maddie gave John another pleading look. This wasn't a great start to their mission. She wiped her mouth with a napkin, pushing away from the table.

"Thank you for having us for dinner. We really should be going," she politely said.

"Yep," Murphy growled.

Maddie tugged on John's hand until he took a step back.

John tossed his napkin on his plate. "Have a good evening," he said before leaving the house.

Charlie and Sandy followed them out on the porch. Maddie and John apologized once again and promised Charlie they would see him tomorrow. They met up with the rest of their team and checked into a hotel a few blocks away.

As John filled the others in, Maddie sat on a bed, absentmindedly twirling a few strands of her hair around her finger.

"Maddie!" John called to her.

"Huh?" She dropped her hand, looking over at him as he leaned against the hotel room dresser.

"I called to you several times."

"Sorry. Lost in thought."

"I can see that." He grinned.

"What are you thinking about so hard?" David asked.

"Balise told me before we left that the Synth kill Charlie in 1965, but don't show themselves to take over the Earth for five years. He couldn't give me any more information other than that," Maddie explained.

"Couldn't, or wouldn't?" Chris asked.

Maddie nodded. "I think that's a fair question."

"I'm not following." John shook his head.

"You're thinking this has all happened before," Chris said.

"Yes, and we failed," Maddie said.

"What makes you say that?" Seth asked.

"It's just a feeling. Something Balise said."

"I need something more to go on than a feeling," Jackson told her.

"I respect that, but when has my gut instinct been wrong?" Maddie responded.

"She's normally right," John concurred.

"What do you suggest?" Jackson questioned, crossing his arms over his chest. His eyes seemed to cloud over as he looked agitated at her.

Maddie didn't mean to make Jackson defensive or to seem like she was challenging his authority. She bit her lip, lowering her head slightly. Truth was, she hadn't fully formulated a plan yet, but she couldn't tell him that.

"Obviously, keeping Charlie alive is our first priority. I wish I knew more. However, I do think our new weapons are key," she began.

The room fell silent. Everyone stared at her. She chewed on one of her fingernails, letting her mind wander. After several minutes, Maddie snapped her fingers together excitedly.

"I figured out a way to keep tabs on Charlie," she exclaimed.

"I'm listening," Jackson pressed his lips together in a thin line.

"What if I make a communicuff for him? Decorative, of course. It would have a tracker in it. I can make it so if he activates it, we can find him as well as hear what's going on."

"Out of the question," Jackson objected, shaking his head.

"Why not?" David asked. "It's ingenious."

"It's too risky. If we're found out -"

"Jackson, I'm not going to let that happen. I can do this," Maddie insisted.

"Charlie does trust her completely," John agreed.

"This is me we're talking about, all right? You really think I would do something that would risk off of our lives?"

"All right, but this is on you if it fails," Jackson stubbornly muttered.

"You are not going to regret this," Maddie said, getting up from the bed.

"See to it I don't."

#

Maddie and Chris went to several different local hardware, electronic, and craft shops to get everything they needed. They spent several hours at work, but once they were done, the communicuff looked like a hand-crafted watch. Maddie wove fabric over the metal to add to the illusion. She also decorated hers and John's in the same manner.

"See?" Maddie held it up for Jackson's approval.

After studying it for several moments, Jackson nodded.

"I still don't like this plan, but it looks good," he admitted.

Maddie and Chris high-fived each other, thrilled with their work.

Everyone went to bed, but hardly anyone slept. Anxiety seemed to hang in the air. The meeting with Charlie was critical to maintain his trust.

"Everything feels fragile," Maddie whispered as she cuddled with John.

"It's not, sweetheart."

"If you or I say the wrong thing …"

"That's not going to happen. We're both too careful to slip."

"Yeah." She snuggled under his chin. "I don't know what I would do if you weren't here with me."

"I'll always be here, Maddie, but I know what you mean."

She placed a closed mouth kiss on his neck. "Words don't describe."

John chuckled low in her ear. "Every damn day, Madison. I love you more with every passing day."

#

After breakfast, John and Maddie met up with Charlie in his garage.

"I have something for you," Maddie said, pulling out the communicuff from her pocket.

Charlie's eyes lit up as he ran his fingers over the braided band.

"This is so cool!" he exclaimed.

John held out his wrist. "See, we each have one."

"I love it! I'm never gonna take it off." Charlie happily danced as he connected the band to his left wrist.

"It's also very special. If you're ever in trouble again, hit this button," Maddie told him, tapping on the button the side. "And we'll come running."

"Why would I be in trouble?" Charlie questioned.

"Well, you were when we met," Maddie pointed out.

"Oh, right," Charlie mumbled, his ears turning pink.

"Just promise me you'll hit the button if you are in trouble."

"I will."

Maddie relaxed her guard as Charlie continued to admire his new accessory. Her chest swelled with pride. Her plan was going to work.

"Would you like to see what I'm working on?" Charlie asked.

"I would love that." She nodded.

Charlie's grin grew as he pulled Maddie over to a work bench. John stood off to the side with his hands in his pockets. Maddie looked over at him then nodded toward a stool in a corner.

"All right, I can see when I'm not wanted." John winked at her. He pulled out a drawing pad from his jacket and kept himself occupied.

Charlie pulled down a box overflowing with random parts from a shelf and handed her a crumbled piece of paper that had a hand-drawn schematic on it.

"What do you think?" he asked.

"It has promise," Maddie answered after a minute of looking over the boy's work.

"You really think so?"

"I do. I also think you'll get it to work."

"Glad you believe in it," he murmured sullenly.

"I believe in you.

He looked up at her, his brown eyes filled with admiration.

"Thanks, Maddie."

"Charlie, why don't you have confidence in yourself?"

"When you're used to hearing that you'll never amount to anything, you start to believe it."

Maddie nudged him before wrapping an arm around his shoulders. "You will. I have faith in you. You need to believe in yourself, Charlie."

Her words seemed to brighten his mood. He smiled warmly at her. He tapped on the schematic. "Want to help?"

Maddie ran her hand along the crumbled up paper to smooth out the wrinkles. From the corner, John cleared his throat warningly, but didn't say anything.

"This is yours, Charlie. I really think you'll do it on your own, and you'll be better for it." She chewed on the inside of her cheek. "But… maybe a few pointers."

John's head snapped up from his drawing pad. They make eye contact as Maddie grabs a pencil from a cup on the work bench. Charlie's eyes lit up as he gave her a blank piece of paper. She drew a crude outline of the original schematic, and then made a few modifications out to the side.

"Forgive my drawing. I'm not the artist John is," she said, showing Charlie her work.

"No, it's okay. I see what you did," Charlie replied, concentrating hard.

"I'll leave you to it. See you tomorrow?"

"Yeah, thanks," Charlie absentmindedly said, pushing his glasses up the bridge of his nose.

John held up his pad, showing of a beautifully detailed picture of her and Charlie. He gave her a thumbs up and motioned for them to leave the garage.

"I think I got it!" Charlie exclaimed as they left.

"What did you do?" John whispered.

"Don't worry about it." Maddie smiled broadly as she grabbed a hold of John's hand and walked down the driveway.

# #

The team gathered in the hotel room to discuss their next course of action. John filled them in on their meeting with Charlie.

"Sounds like it went well," Jackson noted.

"Yeah. It's Charlie, no matter the age." Maddie grinned.

A silence lulled in the room. Chris and David sat in a corner, playing checkers. John sat with his drawing pad on his knee. Maddie sat on one of the beds, staring at the TV. Jackson sat on the dresser, rearranging the supplies in his pockets. Seth stretched out on the other bed, staring up at the ceiling.

"I feel like we should be doing something right now. For the life of me, I can't think of what that would be," Seth said, frustration seeping in his voice.

"I know what you mean. This waiting around is driving me crazy," David agreed.

"Just be ready to spring into action at any moment," Jackson said, eyeing both men.

"Revised history states Charlie will be killed before he activates the device," David pointed out.

"And now, with Maddie's help, that could be as soon as tonight," John said.

"I still disagree with your decision to do that," Jackson groused as he closed the magazine in his handgun. "We don't know what kind of ramifications we're facing due to your interference."

"Jackson, we're already trespassing where we don't belong. Charlie just needed a push, which I gave him." Maddie shrugged. "I provided him the confidence he needed to figure it out on his own."

"What an odd choice of words," Chris commented.

Maddie's face turned bright red as she nibbled on the inside of her cheek.

"What exactly did you do?" Jackson demanded.

"Nothing," Maddie admitted. "I literally just rearranged his schematic. Sometimes a fresh perspective can make all the difference in the world."

"You mean, like a puzzle?" Seth sat up on the bed and asked.

Maddie nodded. "Exactly."

"You're a genius." John looked at his wife adoringly.

"I know." she grinned.

#

Several days went by without incident. Jackson had ordered the team to stay out of public eye to avoid any kind of disturbance. The team tried to occupy themselves with card games and TV but entertainment in 1965 was considerably lacking. Chris laid out on one of the beds, tossing a baseball he found lying in the parking lot in the air. He kept switching from bouncing it off a wall and the ceiling until Jackson snatched it from him and threw it outside. Everyone was going a little stir crazy.

"If I have to watch one more episode of Addams Family, I might snap," Seth complained.

"You shut up! Addams Family is great," David snapped.

"Anything is better than Ozzie and Harriet," Chris chimed in.

"Does anyone else find it weird The Andy Griffith Show is in black and white?" David questioned.

"Everything is in black and white," Chris muttered. "It's 1965, what else did you expect?"

"All right, guys. That's enough." Maddie intervened.

"Maddie, can't you light a firecracker under the kid? I'm ready to go home," David complained.

Jackson, Maddie, and John sat at a small table in the corner, playing cards. Jackson looked up over his hand, rolling his eyes.

"You guys are nothing but a bunch of whiners. You should've been with Mack and me on PS-5730 when we were stranded for two weeks after a crash landing." Jackson chuckled at the memory as he shuffled his cards around. He hummed under his breath for a moment, looking jovial for the first time in a while.

Maddie and John visited Charlie several times, but he was too engrossed in his experiment to pay too much attention to the couple.

"Hey, bud." Maddie pulled up a stool next to Charlie. John stood off to the side, looking aloof.

He didn't look up as he put in place one of his homemade connectors. "Hey."

"This is coming together nicely."

"Yep." He reached over her to grab a metal casing.

"Need any help?"

"Huh?" He finally looked up, blinking several times. "Oh, Maddie, I'm sorry. I wasn't really listening. What did you say?"

She smiled. "Nothing."

"Okay." Charlie grinned. "I'll see you later."

"Dismissing me so soon?" Maddie playfully asked. "I was hoping we could get lunch."

"Maybe later. I really want to work on this."

"All right, Charlie. Call me if you need anything."

Before they left, Sandy gave them a brief tour of the house and apologized to them over her husband's behavior over the dinner they had. Maddie smiled warmly as she offered them lemonade. Sandy reminded her a lot of her own mother. The image of her parents popped in her head as she left the house. She wouldn't fail them.

#

Later that night, the team was asleep when Maddie's communicuff started beeping.

"Shut it off," John groaned, nuzzling against her.

Maddie grumbled, snuggled up against his chest, but the beeping continued. They both shot up like a rocket from their bed.

"Charlie." Worry washed over her in waves as she kicked the covers off of them.

CHAPTER THIRTEEN

The group quickly descended on the quiet suburban home in search of Charlie.

Jackson had previously agreed to set up a perimeter around the house since Charlie wouldn't know him. They all had their orders. John and Maddie were tasked with finding and protecting the teenager. The others would search the house and grounds for the communications device. The house was completely dark as John and Maddie entered the unlocked front door. They exchanged worried glances.

A quick search of the first floor came up empty. They moved swiftly up the flight of stairs. Maddie ducked into Charlie's bedroom while John checked on his parents.

"They're dead," John informed her in the hallway. "Killed in their sleep." John frowned. "I don't think they knew what happened."

"There's no sign of Charlie," Maddie stated.

"You sure that's his room?" John asked.

"Sandy showed it to me the last time we were here when I couldn't get Charlie away from the work bench," Maddie replied.

"Maddie?" Seth's voice crackled over the comm.

"Go ahead."

"The device isn't in the garage."

Maddie and John exchanged nervous looks. She couldn't be sure if it was a good thing or not.

Movement down the hall caught Maddie's attention. Concentrated laser fire whizzed by John's head, missing him by inches. John and Maddie returned fire, blasting a hole in the wall before killing one of the creatures firing at them.

It occurred to Maddie that she hadn't seen their enemy before now. The Synth were hideous, green-skinned creatures. Over seven feet tall and lanky, they had oversized jowls and large eyes that stuck out from the side of their heads. Their limbs moved like rubber bands, bouncing in place.

A blaster shot landed near her feetand knocked her back into Charlie's room. She gave herself a quick once over to make sure she wasn't bleeding before scrambling to her feet. She flicked on the light, giving the room a better scan. Out of the corner of her eye, she saw the lid of a cedar chest close.

"Charlie?" she whispered. "It's okay, Charlie. It's just me."

"Maddie?" His voice came quietly from the chest.

"It's okay, we're here," she said, coaxing him out.

In the box with him was the device he'd been working on. Maddie felt relieved to see a green light flashing on it. Part of their mission was complete. The device was active, and Charlie was still alive. Maddie promised herself neither of those facts would change.

Charlie crawled out of the cedar chest and wrapped his arms around her neck. Maddie could feel his tears flow as he pressed his face into her.

"You did great, Charlie. I've got you now," she soothingly said.

"Mom ... Dad ... What's happening, Maddie?" he asked.

"It's a lot to explain. Let's get you some place safe."

"Thank God, you're okay," John said, rushing into the bedroom.

She managed to unwrap Charlie from her long enough to embrace her husband. After they pulled apart, she took the communication device from the cedar chest.

"We're okay." She pulled a cloth bag from one of the pockets of her pants, dropped the device in, and tied the strings to her belt.

"The floor has been cleared, Maddie. We need to move while we can."

"Charlie, stay close behind me." Maddie gave his hand a squeeze.

The young boy gulped, his eyes filling with fresh tears. Still, he nodded.

Her heart slammed against her ribcage as she checked to make sure her weapon was loaded with the neuteroilum bullets. John searched her eyes until she let out a deep breath, steeling her nerves. She had to remain strong for Charlie, regardless of how she truly felt. This could be the last time John and Maddie were together alive. Judging by the desperate look in his eyes, John knew it, too. She gave him a weak smile before sucking in her bottom lip. John pulled her lip free.

"I love you," he said, brushing his lips against hers briefly.

"I love you, too. Always and forever, John." She wrapped an around his waist, nuzzling his chest. He rested his chin on her head as she closed her eyes, listening to the sound of his heart beating.

"Forever doesn't begin to describe, Madison."

John led the way as they carefully made their way down the stairs. Keeping their back to the wall, Maddie quickly changed the magazine in her gun to normal bullets.

"What are you doing?" John curiously asked.

"The laced bullets are extremely limited. Something tells me to hang on to my mag."

"Good idea."

They could hear blaster fire as they continued their movements. Debris was scattered all over the once spotless living room. Plaster canvassed the brown couch, material missing from the arm rests. Broken glass from the TV and a window littered the orange shag carpet. Picture frames lay on the floor. A huge hole existed where the kitchen used to be.

"Come in, John," Jackson's voice came over the cuff.

"Go ahead." John pulled them to a stop.

"What's your status?"

"We've got Charlie, and the device is green."

"Thank God. That's so much better than my news." Jackson paused. "We lost Chris."

John and Maddie fell silent at the news until Charlie tugged on the back of Maddie's shirt.

"Who's that?" he asked.

"A friend," Maddie told him.

"Seth and David?" John asked.

"They're hurt, but here. What's your location?"

"We're in what's left of the kitchen."

"Very good. We're by the garage. Someone must've called the police by now. We've got to get out of here."

"Understood," John said, signing off.

"What's going on? Who was that?" Charlie questioned.

"It's tough to explain," John replied, looking around the corner to make sure they were still safe.

"Try," Charlie pleaded.

"Wait until we're safe, and I promise you, we will," Maddie assured him.

Charlie grabbed on to her hand as another explosion rocked the house. The structural integrity was compromised as pieces of the ceiling began falling around them.

"Get the hell out of there!" Jackson's voice screamed from their wrists.

The walls started breaking away from the ceiling. The ground shook, the remaining furniture becoming crushed under the sheet rock. A large chuck of ceiling fell from above them. Maddie tackles Charlie out of the way, becoming separated from John in the process.

"Maddie, run!" John yelled over the smoke and debris.

"No, I'm not leaving you!"

"Maddie, please!"

Another explosion rattled the house and cut off John's words. The former residence couldn't take much more abuse. Support beams fell around them, raising clouds of dust as they slammed into the floor. Maddie barely had time to dodge one, avoiding being crushed. She heard a painful cry from John before everything went silent.

"John?" Maddie called.

There was no answer.

When the smoke cleared, only ruins were left. The roof had completely caved in from the kitchen where John had been standing. Maddie's stomach twisted from the fresh smell of blood mixed with the sulfur from the drywall filled the air.

"No!" Maddie shrieked. "John!"

She sank to her knees, tears mixing with the dirt around her eyes, making it burn. She jumped as she felt skinny arms wrap around her neck. Charlie.

As painful as it was, she still had a job to do, or neither of them would survive. She managed to collect herself from the floor, leading Charlie as they dodged the remains from the house. They barely made it to the front lawn when the rest of the roof completely caved in. She put her hands on her knees, trying to cough the dust out of her lungs. She spit to get the metallic taste of sulfur out of her mouth, trying desperately to breathe in clean air.

The Westlake home wasn't the only scene of devastation. The battle had gone past the house, causing chaos and destruction in its wake. She was only barely aware of a strong pair of hands on her shoulders, lifting her to a standing position.

"The Synth retreated to their ship once the neighbors hit the street," Jackson said.

All she could do was nod.

"Maddie, for a second ...Where's John?"

She couldn't answer. The words wouldn't come. Instead, she sobbed into Jackson's shoulder.

"Oh, Maddie." Jackson gripped her tighter, giving her the fraction of a release.

She looked over and watched Seth and David limped over to them. Both men were bruised and bloody, but Maddie didn't care. She pulled out of Jackson's grasp and walked into Seth's outstretched arms. She held Seth as tight as she could before Jackson called to her.

"I'm sorry, but we've got to move," he softly murmured.

Seth looked back at the destroyed house mournfully before nodding. He wrapped an arm around Maddie's waist and the group slowly began to walk away.

Thankfully, the families fleeing the destruction hid Maddie and the others among the crowd. No one seemed to paid attention to them as David broke a window and entered, unlocking the front door of an empty house a block away.

#

Police sirens and cries from the onlookers filled the air outside their new shelter.

Seth got down on his knees in front of Maddie, clutching her tightly. It was too much for her to handle. Her sobs were hard and broken, tears coming in between gulps. She buried her face in his black hair and neck as he broke with her.

Charlie sat next to them, leaning his head against Maddie. Soft sobs echoed throughout the room. Maddie couldn't tell if the sound was coming from her, Seth, or Charlie. Her mind drifted to John's final moments.

She didn't want to feel anything anymore. She wanted to go to sleep and find out it was all a bad dream. But it wasn't a dream. Maddie couldn't escape the reality as it crashed around her shoulders.

"Maddie," Jackson gently called. "I'm sorry, but --"

"No, Jackson," she defensively said, her entire body shaking. "Don't tell me to pull it together. I just lost my husband."

"And I lost my wife!" Jackson snapped. "But we're on a mission, Madison. Time for mourning comes later."

"Can you just give us ... five minutes?" Seth asked.

Jackson grabbed Seth by his collar, yanking him to his feet. Seth didn't struggle or move when Jackson reared his fist back. Time seemed to stand still as Maddie helplessly watched the scene unfold.

"Jackson, we're family!" she shouted.

The punch wasn't thrown. He dropped his defensive stance. He pulled Seth for a brief hug and patted his cheek.

"I'm sorry." Jackson's voice was hoarse.

Maddie stretched out her arms and Seth rejoined her on the floor. They crumbled together in their cries. The weight of it all hit hard. Any loss of their brethren was tough, but under these circumstances, the odds of success now seemed insurmountable.

"I'm so sorry, Maddie," Charlie whimpered, curling his knees to his chest.

"Oh, Charlie." Her voice trembled. "I'm sorry, too."

Maddie took a deep, cleansing breath as she wiped her face on her sleeve. Seth pulled away, beginning to compose himself. Jackson and David joined them, creating a circle on the ground.

Jackson met Maddie's eyes and nodded toward her. Charlie had been promised an explanation, and it would be better coming from the one person left he trusted. She took the boy's hand, giving it a comforting squeeze.

"What I'm about to tell you is going to be difficult to explain, hard to hear, but the absolute truth. Do you trust me?"

Charlie nodded. "With my life."

Maddie held back the smile she felt tugging at his earnest.

"This is Jackson, Seth, and David," she introduced the men in turn. "Charlie, we're from the year 2015. We've come back in time to stop an ancient alien race called the Synth from killing you and taking over our planet."

She had expected him to take a minute to process her words or call her a liar. Instead, he took her by surprise when he nodded.

"Why me? Why am I at the center?" the boy questioned.

"The device you created is extremely important to our future," she said, patting the bag on her hip.

"My communication device?" He stretched out his legs as he turned his body completely toward her.

Maddie nodded. "In our history, your creation catches the attention of a benevolent race known as the Isgurd. Through a friendship with the Isgurd, an alliance is formed into an organization called the Intergalactic Security Commission."

"We all work there," Seth chimed in. "And you are our boss."

"Somewhere in time, our history was changed. The Synth came back to this year to stop you from completing your creation. So in this newly created timeline, you never met with the Isgurd, and the ISC was never formed," Maddie continued.

"So, you are here to ensure I do," Charlie stated.

Jackson nodded. "The future of our planet depends on it."

"Well, the device is working, right? So, now we just need to hang in there for the Isgurd to show up," Seth said.

"If they come," Maddie hesitantly corrected.

"Why wouldn't they?" David asked.

"The Synth are in orbit over our planet. Our friends, with their infinite wisdom and technology, aren't strong in a fight," she explained.

"Ah, hell. Now you say something," David despondently muttered.

Jackson stroked his chin. "We've got to get aboard the enemy ship."

"How do you plan on accomplishing that?" Seth inquired.

"I ... I don't know."

The group fell silent. Maddie's mind raced as she tried to formulate a plan. Jackson locked eyes on her, holding her gaze for several seconds before glancing over to Charlie.

"No. Absolutely not," Maddie said upon realization, emphatically shaking her head.

"What?" Charlie asked.

"I need to use you to lure out the Synth," Jackson explained.

"Are you out of your mind? It's too big of a risk," Maddie objected, throwing a protective arm across Charlie. "If we screw up -"

"Not we, Maddie. You. I need you to protect Charlie while the three of us board."

"Jackson --"

"It's an order, Madison."

"You're out of your mind."

"I'll do it," Charlie interrupted.

"Charlie, no." Maddie shook her head.

The teenager smiled. "I trust you. You'll keep me safe."

"I appreciate the vote of confidence, but -"

"Maddie," Seth's voice cut her off. "You can do this."

"What was it you told me the other day?" Charlie pondered aloud. "You have to believe. I do."

Everyone looked at her, nodding their approval in turn. She sighed, relenting to their team leader's decree.

"Excellent. We'll take a few minutes to prepare, then let's get underway," Jackson said with authority.

#

Mack should be the one here. Not me.

That thought kept popping in Maddie's head. Her counterpart should've been there in her place. Mack would've been strong and ready for anything. All Maddie wanted to do was hide. But there was too much riding on her to fail.

"Maddie?" Charlie pulled her out of her thoughts. "Everything is going to be okay."

She flashed the best smile she could muster, placing an arm around his shoulders.

The team was finishing checking their remaining supplies. Soon, they would leave the safety of the empty house and undergo what should be the final steps in the mission. Regardless of the outcome, this was it.

"What are you thinking?" he asked.

"About my son," she responded without thinking.

"You have a son?"

Maddie nodded. She grabbed the chain around her neck, pulling out the locket. Cracking open the delicate piece, she showed off the picture she had of her, John, and Lucas.

"He's two. Lucas doesn't live with John and me."

"Why?"

"It's too dangerous. Although, I wish I had fought you on it."

"Me?"

"I mean, Future You." Maddie gave the boy a small smile.

"Oh, right. It was my decision?"

"Lucas was safe away from the ISC. But I often regret my decision. I wish I could've come up with something to get you to change your mind."

"Maddie, you really shouldn't be telling him this," Jackson warned.

"Right." She clamped her mouth shut.

"What are the odds I'm going to remember when I'm old?" Charlie offered up.

The team became distracted from the current conversation as the passing of ambulance caught their eye. They watched the police canvass what was left of Charlie's childhood home. Maddie and Seth gripped each other's hands tightly as they watched three black body bags being pulled from the wreckage.

John really is gone. He wasn't waiting until the cops had cleared out to join them like she foolishly had hoped. Much like with Mack, she didn't get a chance to say goodbye.

"I'm the only one left," Seth said, his voice barely above a whisper.

Maddie gave his hand a hard squeeze. The sorrow she felt was different compared to the pain Seth was going through. They grew closer after Logan died and shared a unique bond even for brothers.

"Your brother was very brave," Charlie said to Seth. "He gave up his life for us. I'll never forget that."

"He knew how important it was that we succeed. John did his duty," Seth said, a tear rolling down his cheek.

"Much like Logan," Maddie said.

"Logan?" Charlie looked over at her.

"He was Seth's twin brother. He died two years ago protecting me," she answered.

Seth turned to her, burying his face in her hair. He didn't cry. If he did, there wouldn't be a way to pull himself back together before their next task.

"I know." Her hand stroked Seth's dyed blonde streak away behind his shoulder. "I'm still here. You're more than my brother-in-law. You're my best friend, Seth."

"Maddie," He paused. "Thank God for that."

Once the police were gone, the team waited to see if their green-skinned enemies returned. The aliens eventually rewarded their patience. Six aliens beamed down to the smoldering ruins of Charlie's boyhood home.

"They must have a comm device on them. All we have to do is get one and beam to their ship," Jackson confidently said.

"Oh, yes, all we have to do." Maddie rolled her eyes.

"Everyone but Maddie switch to normal bullets," Jackson ordered, ignoring her. "We'll need to save the special ones for when we board their ship."

The team made sure they were loaded and prepared. Before the three men left, Seth placed his hands on Maddie's shoulders, peering into her eyes. She could plainly see the tears reflecting in his green eyes, mirroring how she felt.

"You can do this, Maddie. I believe in you," he assured her, the sincerity of his words evident in his voice.

Maddie swallowed hard and nodded. Seth kissed her cheek before heading toward the door. A thought popped in her head, making her chuckle. Seth stopped with his hand on the door knob, raising an eyebrow at her.

"No idea why I would think of this, but your sister hates your dyed streak. Says it makes you look like a drunk skunk."

A grin pulled at the corner of his mouth. "Is that a fact?"

"Yep." Maddie nodded. "You should dye it purple. That would really raise her ire."

"Or maybe an electric blue." His eyes danced as he laughed.

"Let's get through this and I'll help you do it."

"You got yourself a deal."

He winked before he flung opened the door and joining Jackson and David. She looked on as they took positions in the shadows, out of sight from their target.

Charlie looked at her as if her head was getting ready to spin off her shoulders. "What was that about?"

"Nothing."

She peeked outside to make sure no one was around. "Stick close to me."

They were still counting on her. Everyone was. This was not the time for failure. Even if it took her last breath, she would succeed.

Maddie slowly took several steps out of the house, motioned for Charlie to follow her. The duo carefully walked to the middle of the street, studying their enemy. The Synth had their back to them. The six aliens were searching around the remaining foundation, looking like they were scanning the materials.

"Looking for us?" Maddie called, firing once as the group turned toward them.

Maddie didn't look to see if her shot met its target. She grabbed Charlie's shirt sleeve and they broke out into a run, dodging blaster shots along the way.

She could hear more shooting, but it wasn't aimed at them. The others must have been executing their plan. Maddie and Charlie made it safely through the neighborhood, coming to the baseball diamond where they first met. She ordered her young companion into the dugout as she came to a stop, turning to stand her ground.

There were only three Synth on their trail now. She hoped the others had accomplished their goal and were aboard the enemy ship by now. She fired twice, shooting one in the chest while the other bullet struck the ground at their enemy's feet, causing a massive energy burst that wiped out the other two Synth. Maddie wasn't close enough to the blast to cause her any physical harm.

"Holy crap, that was lucky." Maddie sighed in relief.

She walked over to the dugout, coaxing Charlie out from under the bench.

"Jackson, come in," she said into her cuff.

Her brow wrinkled up, worry filling her, when he didn't answer.

"Seth, do you read me?"
Still no answer.
"David?"

All she heard was a slight crackle at the other end.

Still nothing.

Maddie felt uneasy, doing the math quickly in her head to see if maybe they wouldn't be able to respond if they were on the ship.

"Maybe they are out of range?" Charlie optimistically said.

"I'm sure that's it," she murmured in agreement, her teeth grazing her bottom lip.

They stayed hidden in the dugout for several minutes before Maddie stuck her head out. Relief washed over her as she saw that the playground was deserted.

"Maddie?" Charlie poked her in the side. "What do we do now"

He asked the question she had been dreading. She had counted on being able to touch base with Jackson by now, if he was still alive. Charlie looked at her expectantly, his large eyes pleading for reassurance.

She grabbed his hands and gave them a gentle squeeze. "We're going to be okay."

She meant to say something inspirational. She wanted to sound like a leader, like Jackson or Mack. Before she could finish her thought, they were both engulfed in a blinding, white light.

# #

"Greetings," a familiar, monotone voice said.

Relief washed over Maddie. They had done it. They were aboard an Isgurd ship.

"Please do not be frightened. I mean you no harm. My name is Balise. You are now safe."

Maddie had to resist hugging the little gray alien, remembering Balise didn't know her. Charlie looked at her then to the Isgurdian, his eyes wide in astonishment.

"Are you the one who contacted us?" Balise asked, his eyes on Maddie.

"I did," Charlie spoke up, his voice shaking from a mixture of excitement and nerves.

"We had ignored your planet for a number of years, thinking your species was too primitive. However, you prove a worth beyond what we thought you were capable of."

"Th - thank you," Charlie stuttered.

"We have much to discuss," the alien began.

Maddie stepped forward. "Starting with the Synth."

Balise slowly turned his attention toward her, blinking a few times before speaking.

"You are not from this time, are you?"

"No, I'm not," she confirmed.

"How did you know that?" Charlie asked, looking over Maddie to see if there was any evidence.

"Balise's kind operates outside normal parameters of time and space."

"Cool," Charlie said in awe.

"This is very strange," Balise said.

"My apologies." She bowed her head slightly in respect. "May I ask if you can read my thoughts?"

Balise rubbed his enlarged head. "It is an ability I am beginning to hone, but I cannot currently."

I knew it! Maddie beamed at him. She quickly introduced them, then filled Balise in on current events. The little alien nodded, speaking occasionally to ask questions. At the end of her story, he offered to help.

"Can you scan the Synth ship for human life signs?" she asked.

"I can." Balise nodded.

They went over to a control panel, pulling up the ship on the screen.

"There are two human life signs, one of which is extremely faint. The ship itself has sustained heavy damage internally," Balise said, as he looked over the scan of the Synth vessel.

"Thank God," Maddie sighed.

Balise rubbed his large forehead as he continued to stare at the screen.

"What's wrong?" she asked.

"There is one life sign."

"I thought you said there were two?" Charlie questioned.

Maddie looked over Balise's shoulder, her heart falling into her stomach.

"There were."

Please, God, let Seth be okay, Maddie prayed. She felt partially guilty about Jackson and David. Seth was her brother. After losing Mack and John, she needed him to survive.

"You said the Synth's ship suffered internal damage," Maddie started, choking back tears. "How extensive?"

"Vast. Sensors show they no longer have weapons or transport. Engines are severely damaged, but operational. Shields are not functioning."

Something tugged in the back of her mind, a memory trying to surface.

"Balise, how long until the ship is operational again?"

"Judging by the extensive damage and limited supplies and technology from your planet, it may take them several years before they will be ready for the invasion you described."

Maddie looked over at Charlie who appeared relieved at the news. The realization from her previous conversation with the Isgurd leader hit her right between the eyes.

"Several years ... we failed," Maddie murmured, feeling crestfallen. Her stomach churned, making her feel nauseated.

"I do not understand," Balise blandly said.

"You told me that Charlie died in 1965, but the Synth didn't take over the Earth until five years later. If time continues from this point, it would make sense in the future. Jackson and the others hurt it, but the ship still stands. The Synth still took over. We failed."

"Except now we have an advantage," Charlie said.

"Precisely. We know what's going to happen. We have the opportunity to stop this once and for all."

"What do you propose?" Balise asked.

"Get me over to that ship. I'm going to finish this."

CHAPTER FOURTEEN

It would take time to change the Isgurd transporters to accept human DNA. It would go much faster this time since she was more familiar with their Isgurd systems. At least time was on their side.

"Have you considered the possibility that you've done this before and failed?" Charlie asked while she worked on the math to assist in the conversion.

"Of course, but it's different this time."

"You have no way of knowing that, Maddie."

"It's ... a feeling."

"A feeling?" he questioned. "A feeling," his tone was harsher.

"Trust me, in forty-eight years, you'll learn to trust my feelings."

"Maddie, what aren't you telling me?"

She set the notebook down and looked up at him.

"You're too smart for your own good," she sighed.

"I've been told that before," he responded, still looking at her for an answer.

"You're going to have to trust me, Charlie."

"I do, which is why we're here."

He looked into her eyes, searching for the missing piece of the puzzle. He felt sick to his stomach when he saw something flicker before she turned away.

"You're not planning on coming back," he gasped.

"No, I'm not. This is a one way trip," she admitted.

The problem, she decided, was they were laboring under the idea they would go back home after their mission was complete. None of that really mattered. All that was important was the Synth were stopped and Charlie survived. She couldn't explain it, but she knew she was right.

"Charlie, listen to me," Maddie started, her tone urgent, as she placed her hands on his shoulders. "If I'm successful, we will see each other again."

"How can you be so sure?" he asked, wiping a tear away.

"Because it's 1965. I won't be born until 1982," she replied with a small smile.

Charlie's eyes lit up. "That's true. Stop the Synth and the timeline will be restored."

"Precisely," she said, brushing a fresh tear away.

Her heart swelled, thinking about John. However, her success wouldn't change what happened with Mack. Unless ...

"I need you to do me a favor, Charlie."

"Anything."

She proceeded to fill him in on Mack, going into details about their history and her counterpart's death.

"Clones? Cool!" Charlie exclaimed.

"Pay attention, Charlie. This is important," Maddie pressed.

"I'm sorry. You want me to make sure the switch doesn't happen."

"No, that needs to happen. I just don't want to know about it."

"I don't understand," Charlie said, tilting his head to the side in confusion.

"There is no way to know how my future would change. Honestly, I don't want it to."

"Okay, I get that. What do you want me to do?"

"Don't ask me to look into the cloning program. At least, not extensively. I want everything as it was before my assistant and I did the blood tests."

"I promise," he vowed.

#

The transporter update was completed several hours later. Maddie had Balise check for life signs once again, exhaling a sigh of relief when he confirmed one human life sign. He informed her there didn't appear to have any other signals near it.

"Thank you, Balise, for everything," she said.

"Madison, best of luck."

She turned her attention to Charlie who looked conflicted. His wrinkled brows highlighted the worry in his blue eyes. Tears looked like they could fall at any moment as his lips trembled.

"I won't fail," she vowed, the confidence clear in her voice.

Charlie nodded before wrapping his arms around her waist, burying his face into her stomach. His hand clinched the back of her shirt as he breathed her in. She reassured him one more time, patting him gently on his back. She kissed the top of his head, ruffling up his hair. His nails scratched her skin as he reluctantly pulled away.

"I don't want you to go."

"I know, Charlie. But I promise everything is going to be okay."

"All right." He had a hard time choking out the words.

"See you soon," she said as cheerfully as she could muster, lightly touching his chin.

She waved at them once, and then Balise beamed her over to the Synth ship in the vicinity of the lone human life sign. She looked around what appeared to be a storage locker. It looked remarkably similar to one of the empty rooms on the ship. The air was chilly. A bright light hung in the center of the room. Several barrels, crates, and bags littered the area. Out of the corner of her eye, something moved in the corner.

"It's me." She held her hands out to show she wasn't armed.

"Maddie?" Seth came out of the shadows. He slowly lowered his weapon, his green eyes wide in disbelief.

"Oh, thank God!" Maddie pulled him into her arms, holding him tightly. He seemed too stunned to move for several moments before slowly wrapping his arms around her. For a moment, everything seemed to pause. They were all the other had left. The realization washed over both of them, causing them to grip tighter. When Seth finally pulled back after several quiet moments, studying her face with curiosity.

"How did ...Where ...What?" he stammered.

"You have such a way with words, Buddy," she lightly teased.

His normally brilliant green eyes shone only a glimmer of her usually upbeat brother-in-law. He gripped her arms, looking her over to make sure she was all right. He seemed to slowly return to his usual self as he playfully smacked her arm before hugging her again.

"Are you okay?" she asked, looking him over.

"Just a few bumps and bruises. Nothing that won't heal."

"Seth!" Maddie's hand covered her mouth as she was overcome with elation that he was all right. Seth chuckled as she hugged him for a third time.

"I'm okay, little one. It's a relief that you're here and not hurt. I'd been going out of my mind with worry ever since we fell out of communications range. You being here must mean you were successful."

"Yep, Charlie is with the Isgurd."

"At least you have good news."

"What happened?"

His eyes darkened. "Jackson devised a plan to cripple the ship. David was going to disable communications, Jackson was supposed to take care of weapons, and I was going to take out the engines. Haven't heard back from David, but Jackson and I made it to the rendezvous point."

Seth pointed to the corner of the storage locker. Maddie could make out the outline of Jackson's body inconspicuously hidden around supply crates. If she wasn't looking for him, she doubted she would've seen him.

Maddie walked over to the corner and knelt down beside his body. Sorrow tore at her heart as she saw the lifeless body of her friend. Dried blood was caked on his uniform from blaster holes in his abdomen and side. His dark hair seemed to frame his head like a halo. His eyes were still open, his right hand resting on his heart. She bowed her head in prayer briefly before gingerly reaching up to close his eyes for good.

"I am so sorry, Jackson," Her voice broke under the weight of her emotions as a tear fell.

"He died not long after I met up with him."

"There's too much of that going around." She swallowed hard as she stood up and walked back over to him. Seth's handsome features were distorted as he mirrored her expression.

"What's your plan?" he asked, tearing his eyes away from the corner.

"We need to blow up the ship."

Seth stared at her blankly for a moment, brushing back the dyed streak of blonde hair from his face.

"Blow it up," he flatly said.

"The ship is crippled. Now is our best shot."

"Is the Isgurd going to beam us back?"

Maddie shook her head. "We don't belong in this time, Seth."

"I know," he sullenly muttered. "We have a job to do, don't we? What are you thinking?"

Maddie held up her gun which still had neuteroilum bullets in the mag.

"You think you can blow up the engines with that?"

"It has enough power."

"I barely made it out of engineering in one piece! That place is crawling with those ugly green bastards."

"All we've got to do is fire into the hypercore drive."

"All we have to do." Seth rolled his eyes.

"Do you have a better idea?"

"Well ... no," he admitted.

Maddie carefully removed the magazine, pulling out the remaining four laced bullets and gave Seth two of them. He checked his vest pockets, pulling out a few remaining flash grenades as well as C4.

"We can use this to create a distraction," Seth said.

"Good."

She hesitated for a moment, walking over to Jackson's body and removed his weapon from him and took two more grenades. She felt guilty as if she was stealing from him and apologized profusely, but they needed the extra explosives. She glanced over at Seth, grazing her teeth on her bottom lip. There was no reason to delay, but still they hung back.

"Maddie?"

"Yeah, Seth?"

"I knew you could do it." He flashed the grin that always put her at ease.

Maddie couldn't help but laugh. "I love you, brother. Let's save the future."

"I love you, too, sis. Sounds pretty good to me."

"Where's the engine room?"

Seth pulled out a handheld device from one of the side pockets on his pants. "Jackson found this," he said. The small device emitted a soft blue light as he powered on. A holographic projection displayed, showing the layout of the Synth ship.

"Hate to say this, but this thing is pretty cool. I wish there was a way to tell future you to create something like this."

"Seth," Maddie warned. "Focus on the task at hand. The engine room?"

"Oh, right," he shrugged unabashed. He pointed to a section of the ship and the holographic image highlighted it and brought it to center view. "It's four levels above us. The best way to enter is by an access hatch right here." He pointed to a tube which connected down to the locker they were in. "That's how I got here."

Maddie studied the projection before nodding. "All right, good. Go down two or three floors, and set off the explosives. Then go up three and meet me there."

"You're the boss," he said, entering the hatch.

Maddie sat on a crate, trying to avoid looking in the direction of Jackson's body. The air in the room was stagnate. She pulled a meal pellet out of her pocket and swallowed. No point dying on an empty stomach.

Her thoughts drifted between John and Mack. She hoped she played her cards right by talking to Charlie. It was dangerous to attempt to change the future, but if there was a chance to protect Mack, she was going to take it. The problem was that there would be no way in knowing if she had been successful.

Loud explosions rocked the ship. Seth had detonated the C4. The Synth hollered as they ran past the storage locker to investigate. Maddie entered the hatch, climbing up to the level they had agreed upon before.

She found Seth just inside the access hatch, curled up against the wall of the shaft. He was holding his right arm. Blood seeped through his fingers.

Maddie touched his arm in concern. "Are you okay?"

"I miscalculated how good the Synth's aim was," he replied through gritted teeth.

She hated to ask. "Can you fight?"

Seth winced as he nodded. "Let's go kill these bastards."

They moved swiftly from the duct to the engineering level. Maddie readied a flash grenade, throwing it as soon as she kicked open the access panel. The aliens screamed in shock and surprise, firing wildly around the room. High pitched wailing seemed to mix with the sounds of shots ringing out. Several were killed by their own blaster fire. Bits of computer components littered the ground. Maddie tossed another explosive, taking out more of their targets in the back of the room. The sounds of the fire rang in Maddie's ears as they dodged the blasts, racing toward the engine core. Green laser fire whizzed by her head, narrowly avoiding her. The next shot struck her right arm, blasting a hole in the synthetic skin. Maddie fired one of her laced neuteroilum bullets, creating a huge crater in the floor and killing several Synth. She heard Seth scream as another shot struck him in his injured right arm. One shot struck Maddie in the leg, but Seth pulled her with his good arm to their destination.

In that moment, in the midst of the pain ransacking her body and the screams she heard all around them, Maddie felt peace. Lucas' laugh replaced the ringing in her ear. John's face was in her peripheral vision. It was almost over. Regardless of how the world played out once she pulled the trigger, she would be reunited with John and Mack.

"Together?" she asked, holding out her hand.

"Together."

She held her breath as the Synth began to descend down on them. Seth took her hand in his as they both raised their handguns. A green blaster fire struck Maddie in the chest as they fired their remaining neuteroilum bullets into the core, causing it to explode.

#

Charlie and Balise watched as a bright light emitted from the center of the ship, temporarily blinding them. To Charlie's delight, the Synth's ship started to break apart. The enemy ship exploded in a silent yet violent fashion. Pieces of the vessel started floating toward the Isgurd ship, disintegrating against the shields.

"Yes!" Charlie jumped up with his fist in the air.

A few of the Isgurd in the observation room bowed their heads as what was left of the Synth ship became nothing more than space dust.

Charlie forgot for a moment the mission and looked around to celebrate the victory with Maddie when the realization sunk in. The smile dropped off of his face as he realized Maddie wasn't going to be there to celebrate. She had been on the ship.

"Maddie did it," Charlie whispered in awe. "She really did it."

"She was very brave, Charles," Balise said. "Her actions ensured your kind will have a future. You should be proud."

"Yes." Charlie swallowed hard as he nodded.

He sank down on the floor, bringing his knees to his chest. He's lost everyone he loves because of the Synth. He dissolved into tears as grief overcame him. He cried until he had no tears left in his system and had been completely unaware of the small alien sitting on the floor next to him.

"Balise, what am I supposed to do now?"

"You are supposed to grow, Charles, and live. You will see Madison again one day."

Charlie brushed the tears from his face as he looked into Balise's coal black eyes. "You're right. And this time, we're going to do things differently."

CHAPTER FIFTEEN

"Hey, Boss," Hunter cheerfully greeted Maddie as he entered her lab. "Got the lab results you needed."

"Took you long enough," Maddie grumbled as she took the folder from her assistant.

"What's eating you?"

"Nothing," Maddie snapped. "Just didn't think it would take you hours for a simple analysis."

She looked up to see Hunter watching her. He ran his fingers through his short red hair, sucking on his bottom lip. She tossed the pencil down, folding her arms over her chest.

"What?" she questioned in a hard tone.

"When was John due back?" he asked

"Three days ago," she replied.

"Ah, no wonder you're short. You're worried."

"I know I shouldn't be. Mack is an excellent pilot."

"You know what you need?"

Maddie cut her eyes away and didn't respond.

"You need cuddle time," Hunter said before disappearing from her office.

"What? Hunter!" Maddie called after him.

"Mommy!" Her son, Lucas, exclaimed as he ran toward her.

"My baby!" Maddie wrapped her arms around her blonde haired, blue eyed two-year-old, covering his face with kisses.

"I saw on the info screen that his shuttle just landed. Thought it would be a nice surprise since it was early," Hunter explained.

"Thank you," she said, her face filled with gratitude.

She sat in a chair, hugging her son tightly. Lucas curled up against her, playing with a lock of her long hair.

"How was your trip?" she asked.

"Uncle Seth fell in the lake." Lucas giggled.

"To be fair," Seth corrected. "I was pushed. I didn't fall in."

His twin brother, Logan, trailed behind him. "I didn't push you. Don't be telling a fib." He wagged his finger. "What do we say, Lucas?"

"Fibber!" Lucas clapped his hands together and giggled again. "Uncle Logan beat Uncle Seth in a wrestling match."

"That ... is true," Seth sheepishly admitted.

Logan grinned as he elbowed his brother. "Sore loser."

"Did you behave for your uncles?" Maddie asked her son.

"Uh, huh. I was real good," he replied.

"Lucas caught his first fish," Logan said.

"You did?"

Lucas nodded, stretching out his little hands to show the size.

"So proud of you! Can't wait to tell your daddy," Maddie smiled, kissing his cheek again.

"What do you say, Champ? Want to go get some ice cream?" Seth asked.

"Can I?" Lucas' blue eyes widened.

"All right, but not too much. Don't spoil your dinner."

"Yay!" Lucas jumped off her lap and ran to Seth, taking his uncle's hand.

Maddie leaned back in her chair, sighing contently. Her brother-in-law pulled up a chair beside her.

"You certainly look happy," Logan commented.

"Not really. I haven't heard from John. He should be back by now."

"Don't sweat it. He'll be back soon. Want me to take Lucas when he does so you can have some quality time?"

Maddie looked at him graciously. "That would be great."

"Of course."

Logan walked over to her desk, looking at the various pictures scattered in frames.

"Oh, wow, I remember snapping this," Logan picked one of the frames up, running a finger over the wood.

The picture automatically sprung tears to her eyes. It was taken two years ago before Maddie officially joined the ISC. Maddie, Logan, Seth, and

Will were goofing around and playing Uno while the rest of the team went to confront a rogue agent.

"Will and I had been friends since we were nine. Hard to believe the only thing I have to remember him by is this picture," she sadly said, reaching out to touch it, stroking the frame with one finger.

"He gave his life to save us, Maddie. There's no shame in that."

"I know. I just miss him."

"Dr. Maddie Brooks, you're needed in the hangar bay," a voice over the intercom called out suddenly.

Logan grinned. "Looks like our boy made it home."

"Make sure Lucas gets some real food, not just sugar," she said, giving him a kiss on the cheek.

"Go on," Logan encouraged.

She didn't need to be told twice. Maddie practically skipped out of the office.

#

Maddie snuggled up next to John as their breathing slowly returned to normal after their intimate reunion. John kissed her temple, holding her naked body against him.

"You said Logan was keeping Lucas tonight?" John asked, running a free hand over her hips.

"All night," she said, nibbling on his ear.

"Wicked woman," John murmured, rolling her onto her back.

The buzzing from the wall broke them out of their bliss. John growled as he pulled away from his wife, bending down to grab his shorts from beside their bed.

"I'm coming, I'm coming," John bitterly said to the door on the wall.

"No, but you will soon," Maddie said in a sultry tone as she finished getting dressed.

John playfully smacked her butt, then opened the door.

"Commander Levette," John unhappily greeted.

"Agent Brooks, you and Dr. Brooks are needed in the command center," Elizabeth ordered.

"Can it wait? I just got back from a mission."

"No, Agent Brooks. The command center."

Maddie frowned, chewing on her bottom lip. Since Elizabeth Levette, John's sister, had taken over for the retired Charlie Westlake, Maddie hadn't been allowed on missions. Elizabeth didn't think a clone should be on the field, regardless of her previous history. With her Master's in engineering and Doctorate in theoretical physics, she was invaluable to the ISC.

"This must be big if I'm invited," Maddie said.

"You're right. We should get going before our illustrious commander calls again."

As the couple entered the command center, Maddie was surprised to see Charlie Westlake sitting next to Elizabeth at the head of the conference table.

"Charlie!" Maddie rushed over, throwing her arms around his neck.

"It's good to see you, Maddie," he said, giving her a squeeze.

"What are you doing here?" she asked.

"I asked the same thing," Mack said, taking a seat across from their current Commander.

Maddie looked down the table at the team assembled. Mack, Jackson, Seth, Logan, and two she didn't immediately know who introduced themselves as Chris Hicks and David Haywood.

"Take a seat," Elizabeth said. "Let's begin."

"Hello everyone," Charlie greeted. "What I'm about to tell you may be difficult to believe, but it's the absolute truth."

Charlie punched a few command keys on the laptop in front of him, activating a 3-D projector to show a moving image of a green-skinned alien race Maddie had never seen before. The race was tall, thin creatures with long, thin limbs that seemed to bounce when they moved. Their eyes were on the side of their head and there didn't appear to be a nose or ears, but they had a thin mouth.

"What are they?" Maddie asked, completely disturbed by the image.

"This is the Synth," Charlie informed. "They are as fearsome an enemy as we've ever faced."

"And they are on their way here with the intention of taking over our planet and enslaving or killing the entire population," Elizabeth stated coolly.

Only their Commander could say something so frightening as if she was talking about what was for dinner in the mess hall.

"What intel have you received with this conclusion?" Maddie asked, looking up from her data tablet. "I just searched the database for reference on the Synth, and nothing came up."

"These foes aren't in the database," Charlie replied.

"That's impossible. Every piece of information the ISC has ever had is loaded into the database."

"Any information regarding the Synth has been classified until now," Elizabeth said.

"Why?" Jackson inquired.

"Because they've done it before," Charlie replied with a wry smile. "And this is the team that stopped them."

Dear Reader,

Thank you for enjoying this adventure with us. Mirror Image is the first in this sci-fi romance series, with Mirror Shattered following. It's exciting that you've made it through the second in a three book series and we are looking forward to sharing the third, Mirror Reformed, early in 2015.

To tell you a bit more about myself, I have a degree in massage therapy. When I'm not weaving words, I enjoy reading, playing RPGs, hockey, wrestling, and football, and I'm a big sci-fi nerd. I am happily married to my wonderful husband, Brad.

You can find my words, and engage me through facebook at http://facebook.com/KGStutts or at my site http://KGStutts.com. You can also find me as a steady contributor to Independent Writer's Association at http://iwassociation.com.

If you enjoyed the books, please share your thoughts on the site you purchased it from. I would love to hear from you, and reviews are a great way to communicate with other readers too!

I'm looking forward to having you along for the ride in the future!

KG Stutts

www.ingramcontent.com/pod-product-compliance
Lightning Source LLC
Chambersburg PA
CBHW060427180626
46817CB00007B/2699